A Season of Change

A Season of Change

Lois L. Hodge

KENDALL GREEN PUBLICATIONS
Gallaudet University Press
Washington, D.C.

Kendall Green Publications
An imprint of Gallaudet University Press
Washington, DC 20002

Library of Congress Cataloging-in-Publication Data

Hodge, Lois L. R. (Lois L. Redmond), 1928-
    A season of change / Lois L. Hodge.
        p.   cm.
    Summary: A thirteen-year-old hearing-impaired girl feels
frustrated by her limitations but tries hard to assert her
independence.
    ISBN 0-930323-27-0
    [1. Hearing disorders—Fiction. 2. Physically
handicapped—Fiction.] I. Title.
PZ7. H6613Se 1987
[Fic]—dc19   87-18945
                                        CIP
                                        AC

Gallaudet University is an equal opportunity employer/educational
institution. Programs and services offered by Gallaudet University
receive substantial financial support from the U.S. Department of
Education.

Dedicated to my mother, Iva Jones Redmond,
who spurred my interest in literature and writing

A Season
of Change

1

Exhausted from jogging, thirteen-year-old Biney Richmond slumped down on a large, arched maple tree root. This particular tree was her favorite. It stood at the top of the small hill that gradually sloped toward the pond. Using her shirt sleeve, Biney wiped the beads of perspiration from her face. She looked up at the sky from beneath the maple's huge branches and large leaves. The fast moving, dark clouds covered the sun and soon took over the whole sky. Biney watched as lightning flashed between the clouds, and she felt the wind rushing by, turning the leaves into a swirling blur. Just then, the vibration of a thunder clap traveled from the ground under her sandals up through her fingertips resting on the tree.

As Biney breathed in the first sweet smell of approaching rain, she moved from the maple tree to the trail meandering uphill through the scattering of cedar, oak, and maple trees. She hurried along the path that led to her home. The large, round, raindrops falling all around her turned into a driving rain.

Biney held her clipboard tightly against her chest, but

despite her efforts, the greeting card she had just drawn began to curl and wrinkle. When she got home, she ran up the three steps to the L-shaped porch, turned around, and watched the storm. Hail streamed downward, skittering off the porch steps onto the grass. Biney's parents had told her long ago that hail made a loud rat-a- tat sound on the porch, but to her, it was a very faint and faraway sound.

Biney had a severe hearing loss; she couldn't hear people talking, she could barely hear cars going down the street, but she could hear her dad's lawn mower if she stood close to it. When she was little, she had a very slight hearing loss. She had been able to hear people talk, and she learned to talk very well. But every year, her hearing had gotten worse. The doctor had tried different hearing aids, but they didn't help for long because her hearing changed too much. She hadn't worn a hearing aid for several years. She doubted if she would ever wear one again.

Shivering in her wet clothes, Biney walked through the twin doors of the old Victorian house. The tantalizing smell of freshly baked cookies blending with the faint musty smell of the large paneled hall engulfed her. On her way upstairs, Biney saw Maria Phillippi dust mopping the hall floor. Maria dropped the mop and turned Biney's shoulders until the ceiling light reflected on both their faces. Maria pointed to the stairs.

"Look at you! You're dripping," Maria said slowly. "Go put on some dry clothes. I'll be up in a minute."

Biney nodded and gave Maria a *where did you think I was going* look. She ran up the curved oak stairs, two steps at a time, leaving damp handprints on the fleur-de-lis wallpaper above the wooden panels. As she entered her bedroom, she looked out the bay window that faced the maple tree and the pond she had left just a few minutes ago. The hail had stopped, but it was still raining hard.

Biney wrapped a towel around her wet hair and then stripped off her soaked clothes. Maria came in and opened the old-fashioned wardrobe. She pulled out a pair of blue shorts and a light blue knit shirt and handed them to Biney. Then she picked up Biney's wet clothes.

"Maria, *I'll* take care of them," Biney said. "I know how."

"Never mind, Biney," said Maria. "I'll do it."

Maria spread the wet clothes on the hamper near the walk-in closet, then she picked up a hairbrush and handed it to Biney. "Make sure you get all the tangles out," she instructed.

Biney frowned and slumped in her chair in front of the dresser. *"How can I feel grown up when Maria and Mom still treat me like a little kid?"* she thought. *"A few days ago, when I wanted to iron my shirt myself, Mom and Maria acted like it was a big deal. Like I couldn't do it without burning myself."*

Feeling her shoulder tapped, Biney looked up at Maria's lips.

"I am going to start supper," Maria said slowly. "Come down in fifteen minutes. I don't think you want me here."

"Maria, I just want to do things for myself," replied Biney. "Can't you see that? You're treating me like I was seven years old."

"Oh, come on, Biney," Maria responded. "It's not that at all. We've had a lot of fun doing things together. We're friends. I'll see you downstairs. And hurry; your parents will be home any minute."

Biney watched Maria leave the room. She liked Maria. Ever since Maria had come to stay at the Richmonds, almost two years ago, they had gotten along well. *"It's funny,"* thought Biney. *"When Mom and Dad told me a*

3

foreign student was coming to live with us and take care of Allen and me after school and in the summer, I was worried. I thought we wouldn't be able to communicate. But, we haven't had much trouble. Maria's really nice, even if she treats me like a kid sometimes. I guess we're lucky her parents decided to move here," Biney concluded. "Or else, we would have lost her a long time ago."

Biney examined herself in the mirror. Her long sandy hair hung straight down each side of her face, covering her ears and falling past her shoulders. She grimaced at the heart-shaped dip of her hairline and the freckles on her nose. "I hate these freckles," she said to herself. "And I'm too short. When Mom measured me yesterday, I was only five-feet tall. I wish I was built like Maria; she's so tall and slender. But Maria is nineteen. Maybe I'll grow some more, although I doubt it; everybody in our family is short."

Brushing her hair toward the back, Biney grabbed the strands together with her left hand and studied her face. "One day I'm going to cut my hair short," she told herself. "I'll surprise Mom, Maria, and everybody." Then she turned around a few times, checking her figure in the mirror, and went downstairs.

When she reached the foyer, Biney looked out of the oval window of the front door. The sun was beginning to peek out from behind the clouds, though the grass and trees were still sparkling wet. Moving to the hall mirror, she double-checked her hair. In the mirror, Biney saw her brother Allen walking in the front door with a big grin on his face.

Allen tossed his baseball cap in the air toward the chair by the telephone stand. It missed. Allen stood in front of Biney, hitting his baseball repeatedly against his mitt.

"Biney. We won. We're the champions." Allen announced, dancing a jig. "Hot diggety dog!"

"Great," said Biney. "What was the score?"

"Fifteen to fourteen," answered Allen, still jumping around.

"Hold still," Biney demanded. "Let me see your lips."

Quieting down, Allen faced Biney and began to talk slowly. "It was a close one. I wish I could stay eight years old so I could play in the midget league again next year. Hey, something smells good. Come on. I'll bet we're having chicken. Let's see if supper's ready."

Biney raced Allen down the long hall from the foyer straight into the kitchen. Their mother was standing by the door talking to Maria, who was getting ready to leave.

"Bye, kids," said Maria, making a waving motion with her fingers. "See you tomorrow."

"Bye, Maria. Hi, Mom," they said at the same time.

Mrs. Richmond walked over and hugged her children. "Hi, kids. Am I glad to get home! I was really busy at the bank today. That chicken Maria made smells so good. Are you ready to eat? Come on, what are you waiting for? Biney, go get Dad; he's in the family room. Allen, get out of those wet clothes and see what you can do with those dirty hands."

Biney found her father smoking his pipe in an easy chair next to the fireplace. "Hi, Dad," she said. "Did you have a good trip?"

"Yes, I did," her father answered. "How's my girl?"

"I'm all right," Biney responded. "Mom says it's time to eat."

"I'm ready and hungry," he said, getting up.

Within ten minutes, the family was sitting around the table in the large dining room. "Where did you go this time, Daddy?" Biney asked. "I forgot."

"To Middleburg. Some businessmen up there are starting a new TV station."

"That's up in the mountains," said Allen. "Can they

get a good picture there?''

"It should be okay," Mr. Richmond answered slowly. "A lot of people in the mountains have satellite dishes. They probably get better reception than we do!"

Biney and Allen laughed. "When do you have to go back?" Allen asked.

"Tomorrow, and I won't be back for five days. It will take me that long to set up the tower and make sure it works properly."

Biney looked down at the chicken and potatoes on her plate and realized she hadn't eaten because she had been watching her father's lips. As she picked up the drumstick, she remembered the ruined drawing on the clipboard. She had promised Mrs. Caldwell at the stationery store that she would have twelve cards ready by the weekend. She still had to draw two more.

The motion of her mother's fingers tapping on the table in front of her brought Biney's attention back to the family. *"I wish she would quit that,"* Biney thought as she looked toward her mother's lips.

"Biney. Stop dreaming," her mother was saying. "You know, school starts next week. Both you and Allen need some new clothes, so we're going to the new store at the mall tonight."

"Oh boy!" exclaimed Biney.

"Also, I've been thinking about school this year, Biney. Ninth grade is the beginning of high school. It's going to be a big change for you. You haven't had a hearing aid for several years, and there have probably been some changes because of all the new technology. I went to see an audiologist to find out if there was a hearing aid or some listening device that could help you hear better. I'm going to take you to his office tomorrow."

"Will I hear like you?" asked Biney, uncertain whether

6

she liked the idea of getting a hearing aid.

"You will hear more than you do now," her mother answered slowly. "But, I don't know how much."

"Will I still have to read lips?" asked Biney.

"Yes. Be thankful you can read lips, Biney. You are an excellent speechreader, and most of the time your speech is easy to understand. (*"I'm not such an 'excellent' speech-reader,"* Biney thought. *"I have a hard time understanding some people."*) That's why you've done so well in school." Biney's mother then turned and started talking to her husband and son.

Biney noticed, as she had many times before, how much faster her mother talked to other people. Biney resented not being able to understand her.

"Mom," said Biney. "Mom."

"What, dear?" she answered.

"What were you talking about to Dad and Allen?"

"Never mind, Biney. It wasn't important."

"Mom, I hate it when you say 'never mind.'" Biney got up from the table. *"And I hate being left out,"* she said to herself.

Biney walked into the family room across the hall and slouched in a rocking chair in front of the television. Allen came into the room, turned on the television, and sat in the other rocking chair. On the screen, a man talked rapidly while two boys sneaked up behind him, fingers pressed to their lips.

"Allen, what did the man say?" asked Biney.

"Oh, Biney, it isn't important. It's just an ad."

Biney frowned. *"Another never mind."* "Then it's not important to you, either," she said, pushing in the knob to turn off the television.

"Hey!" exclaimed Allen. "Don't do that!"

Allen jumped up to turn it back on and pushed Biney to

7

keep her away from the television. In the wrestling match that followed, Biney's elbow hit the antique rose vase sitting on top of the television. The vase fell to the oak floor and shattered.

"Look what you did," exclaimed Allen.

"Oh, no-o-o," whispered Biney, stunned.

Biney could not move. Her mother's favorite vase was now lying in pieces all over the floor. Biney blinked back tears as she felt a pull on her arm.

"Go get the broom," her father ordered, moving his hands in a sweeping motion.

Quickly obeying, Biney ran for the broom. When she returned, she carefully swept up the broken glass. Allen carried the dustpan to a wastebasket, tossing in the broken pieces.

"It's time to go shopping," Dad said, pointing to the door. "We'll settle this later."

2

Biney went outside and waited for her parents in the back seat of the car. Looking at their tall old house, she thought of how much she loved the bay windows, especially the way the day's last few sun rays reflected off the windows in her bedroom upstairs and the kitchen nook downstairs.

Biney watched her mother open one of the double doors and step onto the shaded porch. The porch ceiling supported Biney's tiny art room and balcony. Biney's mother motioned to Allen, who was rocking in a swing at the end of the porch. Her father locked the front doors and all three joined her in the car.

As they drove away from the house, Biney rolled down the back windows to let the hot summer breeze rush through the car. She took in the spicy smell of the red cedars lining both sides of the driveway. The long drive ended at a gate suspended between two stone posts. Each post held a big stone milling wheel. Those wheels had been used long ago by her grandparents to grind wheat and corn. Biney barely remembered the empty old mill, which had been torn down when she was five years old. Those wheels were now the only evidence left of the mill.

When they reached the gate, Allen got out of the car, opened the gate, and waited for his father to drive past the posts. Then he fastened the gate and ran back to the car.

For the rest of the drive, the mile to town and the five blocks of the main street to the new shopping mall at the opposite edge of town, everyone was quiet. *"I wonder how Dad's going to punish us when we get home,"* Biney asked herself.

As the family entered the huge shopping center, Biney's mother tapped Biney on the shoulder. "Biney, watch my lips carefully," she said, moving her fingers to her lips. "What do you do if we lose each other and you can't find me?"

"Come here by the door, Mom," answered Biney. "You told me that a long time ago."

"What things are on each side of the door?" her mother asked.

Biney looked around. "Cameras on one side, tools on the other."

"Remember that. There are many doors in this building. It's confusing."

Then Mrs. Richmond spoke to her husband. "Bill, Allen needs some shirts."

"Okay, we'll see what we can find," Mr. Richmond replied. "Have fun, girls," he said as he and Allen left in search of shirts.

"How can we have fun?" thought Biney, remembering again the shattered vase on the family room floor. *"What will Dad do to us?"*

Mrs. Richmond tapped Biney's shoulder again. "Biney, stay close to me."

Biney stepped behind her mother on the escalator that

moved slowly and methodically upward. *"I wish I could go around the store and look for clothes by myself. But, that's another no-no. When will Mom think I'm old enough to do things on my own?"* she lamented.

The second floor of the new store was filled with clothes of all shapes and colors that dazzled Biney as she looked all around her.

"Come on, Biney," her mother said, grabbing her hand as they wormed their way through the clothes.

As Biney waited for her turn to use one of the dressing rooms, her mother brought her more and more clothes to try on.

"Am I going to get all these?" asked Biney.

"Yes, if they fit. Haven't you noticed how much you've grown?" responded her mother slowly, facing Biney.

Half an hour later, Biney carried the pile of clothes to the checkout counter. She was reading the price tags when she saw a woman walk up to her mother and hug her. It took Biney a few seconds to recognize their old neighbor. "Hi, Mrs. Foster."

"Hi, Biney," answered Mrs. Foster, slowly, looking directly at her. "How are you?"

"Just fine, thank you."

"Good. It's nice to see you, again." And then Mrs. Foster turned to talk to Biney's mother.

Biney took this opportunity to pick out an outfit by herself. After pulling out and replacing several blouses and skirts, she fell in love with a long, multicolored shirt. She also found a pair of designer jeans.

"Beautiful," she exclaimed to herself. *"This is it! I must have this outfit."*

All of a sudden, someone covered Biney's eyes. Pulling the hands off, Biney turned around to see who was there.

"Hey, Pat," exclaimed Biney, hugging her best friend. "Did you have a good trip?"

"We had a wonderful time at the beach," Pat answered slowly. "Look, at my tan!" Her blue eyes looked enormous behind her thick glasses.

"Are you looking for school clothes?" asked Biney. "Is your brother here, too?"

"Yes," Pat answered, nodding. "Gene needed shirts. He's been lifting weights." Pat moved her arms up and down, clenching her hands as if doing the lifting herself. "His arms and shoulders are big." Pat moved her hand over an imaginary flexed bicep repeating, "Big."

Biney nodded.

"Come over to my house tomorrow," Pat suggested.

"Okay, I will," Biney answered, nodding. "Do you think your mother would cut my hair? She's a beautician, right? I want it really short."

"How about me?" asked Pat, pointing to herself and moving her fingers as if cutting. "My mom taught me how to do it."

"Great," Biney replied. "Guess what? I might get a hearing aid. But I'm not sure if I want it."

Pat stopped examining a blouse on a rack. Her eyes grew bigger behind her thick lenses. "I wonder if you will be able to use the telephone," she said, placing her hand next to her ear as if holding a receiver.

"No," answered Biney. "How can I read lips through a telephone?"

"Come on, Biney. The hearing aid is supposed to make you hear, isn't it? Don't be so negative. I'm going to talk to you on the phone when you get that hearing aid!"

"No, you're not," responded Biney. She couldn't imagine using the phone. The vibration of it ringing was all she knew about it.

"Just think. We could talk to each other more often if you would use it," Pat said enthusiastically.

"Pat, I can't use it," Biney blurted angrily. "Just forget it."

"Uh oh, I've got to go. Mom's calling me. You'll come tomorrow, won't you?" asked Pat. "I'll cut your hair for you."

Biney wanted to skip it. Talking about a hearing aid had upset her, but she did want her hair cut. Hesitating a second, Biney finally nodded.

"Okay, see you then."

Biney stood a second, wondering if she had made a mistake. She knew Pat would bring up the subject of the telephone again. *"There's no way I'm going to use it;"* Biney thought irritated, *"hearing aid or no hearing aid."*

Biney carried the new outfit over to her mother. "Mom, I want this," she said with a determined voice.

Her mother frowned and looked at her sternly. "Biney, you must not interrupt when I am talking to someone. Understand?"

"That's all right," said Mrs. Foster. "It's time for me to go anyway. Biney, you start school in a few weeks, don't you? What grade are you in?"

"Ninth," answered Biney.

"High school, already! I remember when you were five years old, Biney. You have grown up so fast."

"Yes, I guess so," she responded. *"Why do adults always say that?"* she wondered.

"Well, I must go. Come see me soon. And good luck in school."

"Bye," Biney and her mother called.

"Mom, please buy this for me," said Biney, holding up the shirt and pants. I really like it."

"I don't know about this outfit for school. I don't think

13

it's appropriate. If you really want it, I think you should pay for it.''

"Great," thought Biney. *"I finally get to do something for myself."* "I don't have enough money now, Mom, but I can get it by selling my drawings," Biney said excitedly. "Please let me do it."

"All right," her mother responded. "We will put it on layaway tonight. You know you will have to make a payment every week. When you pay for it in full, then you can take it home."

"Oh boy, thanks Mom," Biney said, giving her a hug.

"You realize you must pay a little each week, or else you will lose it, right?" asked Mom.

"Yes, I know," answered Biney.

"Okay." Biney's mother paid for the other clothes and then said, "Let's go," pointing toward the escalator. "Dad and Allen must be waiting for us."

But they weren't there yet. So, while Biney's mother waited for them, Biney wandered over to the camera counter. *"I wish I had one of these,"* she said to herself as she looked at the different cameras. *"I could do some of my drawing inside if I had photographs to use. I wonder if you can buy cameras on layaway."*

Just then Biney remembered to look to make sure her mother was still waiting at the main door. Her view was blocked by a teenage boy who was staring at her. Biney almost didn't recognize Pat's brother, Gene, because he had changed. His chest and his darkly tanned arms were muscular; Pat had told her that Gene had been lifting weights, and Biney could really see the difference. Her eyes shifted to Gene's lips.

"Hi, dummy," he mouthed silently. He grinned at her and then moved into the crowd of customers leaving the store.

14

Biney frowned and scolded herself. *"Caught again! How can Pat stand her older brother? Gene has bugged me ever since we met. He always calls me 'dummy'. I hate it. But he knows I have to look at people's lips. Why is he so mean to me?"* she wondered.

Biney's father caught her attention by motioning to her to come. "Let's go," he mouthed.

It was dark now, but the air was still hot and muggy. The lights from the houses along the highway reflected off the asphalt. Biney thought about the pond and the woods hidden in the dark. *"Tomorrow, I'll try to finish my drawings at the pond,"* she decided.

As the car passed the red cedars along the driveway, Biney watched a faint white object in front of the house grow bigger. It was a little car, one she had never seen before. Her father parked among the cedar trees a short distance from the strange car. He got out of the car, leaving the lights on, and walked slowly toward the white car.

Mrs. Richmond, Biney, and Allen got out of the car. Biney felt her mother's arm wrap around her waist and pull her, along with Allen, toward the cedar trees. As Biney watched, her father's faint dark outline moved slowly from the white car toward the side of the house and disappeared in the dark. She thought she saw something move near the house, but it was so dark, every bush and tree seemed to be moving.

"Where is Dad?" she asked herself. *"Why isn't he back, yet? Don't get hurt, Dad,"* she prayed over and over. Her throat tightened. Goosebumps raced down her arms. She shivered.

3

Biney could not stop her body from shivering. She squeezed Allen's hand and clung tightly to her mother's waist. *"Where is Dad?"* she wondered. Looking around the frontyard, she could see only the black outlines of the bushes next to the house.

Allen was being very quiet. Usually he couldn't stand still for long. Biney wondered if he was afraid. She couldn't tell whether her mother was afraid, either. Neither one of them was shaking, but she couldn't stop it. The familiar fragrance of the cedar trees around her did not calm her trembling. The twinkling stars of the Big Dipper, which had always seemed close to her, now seemed so far away.

Biney saw the hall light flash on, spreading its light on the porch and the grass in front of the house. Mrs. Richmond pulled Biney and Allen toward the house. Not wanting to see her dad hurt, yet feeling the need to find out what happened, Biney looked into the hall. He didn't look hurt. In fact, he looked all right, and he was talking to someone. Biney couldn't see who it was.

"You look as if you're seeing a ghost, Biney," exclaimed Maria. "You're really pale."

16

Startled, Biney looked at Maria. "You? Is that your car?" She breathed a sigh of relief. "It was dark. I couldn't see. I couldn't hear. I couldn't talk to Mom. I didn't want Dad to get hurt. I was scared." Tears rolled down Biney's cheeks.

"Biney!" Maria exclaimed, wrapping her arms around Biney's shoulders. "I'm sorry. Come on, let's go into the family room. I have something to tell you."

While Biney's father went to turn the car lights off, everyone else moved into the family room. Her mother and Allen sat down on the rose sofa facing the fireplace. Maria relaxed on the other sofa while Biney straddled the footstool facing Maria. When her father came in, he sat in an easy chair on the other side of the fireplace.

Maria faced Biney and talked slowly. "Do you remember a few years ago when I was really sick and had to stay in the hospital for a few weeks? The nurses were wonderful to me, and ever since then, I've wanted to be a nurse, too. I want to help people like they helped me."

Biney nodded.

"To kind of prepare myself, I applied for a job as a nurse's aide," Maria continued. "I start next week. I will have to drive to the hospital, so my dad got me a new car. I couldn't wait to show it to you. That's why I came over. I found the key in the garage and was planning to turn on the lights and wait for you when you pulled in the driveway."

"Does that mean you won't be coming to stay with us anymore?" asked Biney.

"No, I'll still be here," Maria answered. "My job at the hospital is in the evening. I'll be with you after school. By the way, do you need to go to town tomorrow?"

"Yes," answered Biney. "To the library and Mrs. Caldwell's."

"Great," said Maria. "We'll go in my new car. Allen, want to ride along?"

"No, that's okay. I told Jim I'd play with him," answered Allen. "We only have a few weeks left before school starts."

Not watching Maria's lips anymore, Biney began thinking about how afraid she had felt in the dark. She had been really scared. After seeing Maria, she had felt better and was surprised to find herself crying. *"I wonder why I started crying? Everything turned out all right, didn't it? Did not knowing what was going to happen make me cry? Maybe. Now I bet everybody thinks I acted like a baby. No wonder they never let me do anything on my own."*

Biney noticed Maria had turned to talk to her parents. They were talking too fast for Biney to be able to understand the conversation. Her eyes started to drift around the room. All of a sudden, she remembered the vase. *"What is Dad going to do to me for breaking it?"* she asked herself. *"Maybe, if I don't mention it, Dad will forget about it. Or maybe I can find another one to replace it."*

Maria touched Biney's hand to get her attention. "It's time for me to go," she said. "Sorry I scared you, Biney. You're all right now, aren't you?"

Biney nodded.

The next morning, Maria and Biney drove to town in Maria's new car. "I'm not used to the shift, yet," said Maria. "Dad's car is automatic; you know, you just put the car in drive and it goes. I have to get used to shifting gears."

"Oh, so that's why the car jerks," Biney said, grinning when Maria frowned at her.

"Hey, I'll get you for that," exclaimed Maria.

Maria pulled up in front of the library. "I'll meet you at Mrs. Caldwell's," said Biney.

"Never mind, Biney," Maria replied. "I'm going in the library with you. You go on in while I park the car."

Biney wanted to show Maria she knew what to do in the library, so she walked straight to the reference room. She wanted to take out a nature book. She knew they were on the round table in the middle of the room. Looking at the titles, she searched for a book about trees. She looked through the titles again...and again.

"Where are the nature books?" she muttered. "These are all about people."

Not finding what she wanted, Biney walked over to the reference librarian and asked for help. The librarian pointed, said a few words, and rushed off.

Biney followed in the general direction the librarian had pointed and entered a room filled with more reference books. *"I'll never find anything in here,"* she thought, becoming frustrated. She turned around and noticed Maria behind her.

"Come on, Biney. I heard what the librarian said. They moved the books you are looking for to another room."

After looking through several books, Biney picked out a couple to take with her. Maria began to take the books from Biney's hands as they walked toward the checkout counter.

"No, Maria," said Biney. "Remember? I want to do things for myself. Let me check them out."

"All right," Maria replied. "I'll get the car and pick you up in front of the library."

Biney laid her books on top of the checkout counter and placed her library card on top of the books. She wished she could understand what the talkative librarian's lips were saying. When the books were stacked directly in front of her, she picked them up and turned to leave. As she ap-

19

proached the outside door, a man entering the door stopped her, spoke to her, and then pointed to the checkout counter. Puzzled, Biney turned around. The librarian held up her library card. Biney returned to the counter and the librarian handed her the card.

"Thank you," Biney said softly.

Outside on the library steps, Biney watched for Maria. While she was waiting, she saw Pat's brother Gene. He walked directly toward her, but she pretended not to see him. She looked sideways, watching for Maria to approach the curb. After a few minutes, when she was sure that Gene would be inside the library, she peeked back. Gene was standing next to her, waiting.

"Hi, dummy," he mouthed.

"Caught again. If I hadn't looked at his lips, I wouldn't have seen those words," she scolded herself. Looking away quickly, she spied Maria's car. She rushed toward the curb, hopped into the car, and then looked toward the library. By that time, Gene had disappeared into the building.

"What's the matter, Biney?" questioned Maria.

"Nothing," she replied.

"Nothing, my foot," answered Maria. "Something has happened, and it sure has upset you. Don't you want to talk about it?"

"Everything's going wrong," Biney exclaimed angrily. "First, I tried to find the books. When I asked about them, I couldn't understand the librarian. Then, I almost forgot my library card." She paused. "And then, I ran into Gene."

"Give yourself time, Biney," answered Maria. "You're not quite ready to do things on your own. That's why I go with you."

"But, I'm almost fourteen! I have to do things by myself," Biney exclaimed. "You don't know how hard it is to speechread people. Sometimes, I can't understand anything

20

somebody tells me. The only people I can usually under-stand all the time are you, Dad, Mom, and Allen.''

"You have to be patient with people, Biney. And you have to ask them to repeat themselves if you don't under-stand them the first time. Part of that ability comes with maturity. Give yourself some time,'' Maria advised. "What's this about Gene?''

"He called me dummy.''

"Are you sure?'' asked Maria. "Isn't he Pat's brother?''

"Yes,'' Biney responded. "I understood him.''

"Well maybe you misunderstood him,'' answered Maria as she moved the car into the traffic. "Don't worry about it.''

"I wish I hadn't mentioned Gene,'' Biney muttered to herself. *"I knew Maria wouldn't believe me, and she didn't. Nobody knows how Gene torments me. Not even Pat.''*

Maria dropped Biney at the stationery store and ar-ranged to meet her later. Biney entered the small store. It contained several long racks of cards. Bypassing the birth-day, wedding, get-well, and ugly cards, Biney picked up several boxes of plain ones and walked to a small table near the door. She searched through the small cards she had painted for Mrs. Caldwell a month ago. She found only a few left. Biney looked up when she felt someone tapping her on the shoulder.

"Hello, Biney,'' Mrs. Caldwell greeted her. "I'm glad to see you. How are you?''

"Pretty good,'' responded Biney.

"Biney,'' said Mrs. Caldwell, "two of my customers want to buy more of those cards with the drawings of the tree leaves and the cattails. Could you make some more by next week?''

Biney nodded. "I have eight done. I like doing them. I'm saving the money I earn to buy a camera. Real pictures would help me improve the drawings."

"That's a good idea," said Mrs. Caldwell, "but you paint very well even without pictures."

"Thanks," said Biney.

Just then, Maria entered the store awkwardly carrying several large shopping bags. After visiting with Mrs. Caldwell a few minutes, she turned to Biney. "Do you have everything you need? If so, let's go home."

"If you can, Biney, please bring in ten or more cards by next weekend," Mrs. Caldwell requested.

Biney nodded. "I'll sure try. Good-bye, Mrs. Caldwell."

As they drove home, Biney once again admired the old red cedar trees lining the drive between the highway and her old Victorian home. Her grandparents had built the house long ago.

Maria stopped the car in front of the house, turned the motor off, and then turned sideways so that she faced Biney. "Last one in is a rotten egg," she challenged.

"Oh no you don't," Biney shouted.

Quickly pushing the door open, Biney clambered out and raced around the car toward the L-shaped front porch with its spindled rails. She got to the double doors just as Maria did. They both reached for one of the doorknobs, trying to push each other out of the way. As Maria turned the knob and began opening the door, Biney ducked under her arm, pushed the heavy door wide open, and tumbled down on the hall floor.

"Ha, ha, I beat you," said Biney, grinning.

Maria stood in the doorway, her tall, slender body silhouetted against the background of the bright sunlight. She reached down to tickle Biney.

"I'm getting you for this."

22

Biney giggled and reached up to grab Maria's striped blouse. She yanked hard.

With a shriek, Maria toppled over Biney. "You brat," exclaimed Maria.

Out of breath from running and laughing, they leaned against the oak stairs. Biney noticed the grandfather clock, which sat against the stairs, was about to strike. She reached out to the smooth wooden body of the clock. When the long clock hand reached twelve, her sensitive fingers felt the vibrations penetrating the wood. After she had lost her hearing, she had learned to tell time by counting the number of times the wood quivered. She lovingly touched the polished wood of the old walnut clock that had belonged to her grandparents.

"What time is it?" asked Maria.

"It's one."

"It's time to make the cookies then," said Maria. "Or, should we make the pecan pie?"

"Oh, let's make the pie," urged Biney.

For the next half hour, Biney gathered and measured the ingredients while Maria prepared the pie. When Maria had finished the last step of grinding the pecans and spreading them on top of the pie, she placed the pie in the oven and turned on the timer.

"Please wash the dishes while I set the table," said Maria. "You'll be close to the timer."

About forty-five minutes later, Biney put her fingers on the timer and waited until she felt it buzzing. "Pie's ready, Maria," she announced.

"Do you want to take it out? Remember to use the pot holders. It's going to be hot," Maria warned.

"Oh boy," Biney answered. Pulling on the oven mittens, she gingerly reached into the hot oven, pulled out the pie, and placed it on top of the stove.

"Ummm, that smells good!" her mother exclaimed as

she walked into the kitchen. "Wish we could eat it now."

"Why can't we?" asked Biney. "How come you're home early?"

"We have an appointment at the audiologist's office. Remember?"

"Oh, yeah. Do I have to go, Mom?" Biney asked.

"Yes, you do. It's time we found a hearing aid that can help you. Now come on, I don't want to be late."

As the car traveled through the sultry shade of the cedar-lined driveway and entered the highway leading to town, Biney became tense. *"What's going to happen?"* she wondered. *"Will I get a hearing aid today? I probably won't be able to understand the person giving the hearing test. I hardly ever can understand anyone outside the family. How will the audiologist know how much I can hear? I don't see why I have to go; I wish Mom would turn around and go home."*

Fifteen minutes later, Biney was shaking hands with Mr. Wade. She followed him into a small office while her mother stayed in the waiting room. Mr. Wade had a dark mustache and beard that was trimmed away from his lips. Still, Biney thought that he would be hard to speechread.

"Biney, I want to ask you a few questions just to get acquainted," Mr. Wade said slowly. "Then I will test your hearing. Can you hear me?"

"No, but I can read your lips," she answered, relieved to understand most of his words, despite his mustache.

"How old are you?" asked Mr. Wade.

"Thirteen," answered Biney.

"Do you like school?" asked Mr. Wade.

"I did last year," she responded.

"Do you have any brothers or sisters?"

"I have one brother," Biney answered. "His name is Allen."

Then, Mr. Wade put a book in front of his lips. A few minutes later he put the book down on the table.

"Biney, could you hear anything when I had my lips covered?"

"No. Did you say something?"

"Yes, I did," answered Mr. Wade. "You speechread very well. Let's go into the testing room and find out how much you can hear."

They walked down a short hall into a room that was empty except for a table and two chairs. There was a mirror on one of the walls. Mr. Wade showed Biney some headphones that looked like the ones she had seen airplane pilots on television wear.

"Biney, you are going to wear these earphones during the test. I am going to test your ability to hear sounds at different pitches. Each sound will be a little higher in pitch than the one before it. Also, the sound will be very soft at first, but it will become louder. I want you to raise your hand when you hear the sound. I will sit on the other side of the mirror. I will be able to see you from the other room, but you won't be able to see me. That's so you can't read my lips. Do you understand what to do?"

Biney nodded.

Mr. Wade placed the earphones on her ears and left the room. After about a minute, Biney could hear some low tones. She raised her hand every time she heard something. But after a while, as the sound pitch moved higher, she raised her hand less and less often.

After waiting for what Biney thought was a long time without hearing anything, Mr. Wade came into the room and took off the earphones.

"This time, Biney, I am going to say a few words in the microphone. Repeat the word if you recognize it. Don't worry if you don't hear anything."

With the earphones covering her ears again, Biney waited and waited to hear something. Her eyes searched the semidarkened room. She noticed some pamphlets on the table. Biney picked up one and looked at the picture on the cover. She felt isolated and forgotten in the tiny room.

Suddenly, she heard, "Biney."

"Hey, I heard that...'Biney,'" she exclaimed. Alert now, she closed her eyes to concentrate better. But she could not understand the words even though she kept hearing some sounds.

Mr. Wade returned to the room and removed the earphones. "Come back into the office now, Biney," he said.

Biney came in and sat in the chair near Mr. Wade's desk. Her mother, who was already in the office, gave her a reassuring smile. Biney watched Mr. Wade's face closely. She wanted to ask him why she couldn't understand anything except her name. She became disappointed and discouraged when Mr. Wade began to talk to her mother instead of to her. Always before, Biney had accepted the fact that she had to wait to learn what was said by talking with her mother, later. This time, she wanted to hear directly from Mr. Wade. She tried to concentrate on what he was saying, but she couldn't understand him. *"Why doesn't he talk to me?"* she asked herself. Biney shifted in her seat and gritted her teeth to keep from asking questions.

Finally, Mr. Wade turned to Biney. He picked up a lump of clay and spoke slowly to her.

"I'm going to make an earmold from this clay, Biney. First I will warm it to soften it, and then I will place a piece of it in your ear. I'll put cotton in your ear first, so the clay will not go in too far."

While the clay was being warmed, Biney watched Mr. Wade as he talked rapidly to her mother. Unable to understand him and feeling resentful at being left out, she wanted to interrupt him and find out what he was saying. But, she didn't dare. Her mother had scolded her often and told her to be quiet when others were talking.

Biney sat quietly while Mr. Wade put the cotton and warmed clay in her ear. When the clay had cooled, he pulled it out and said, "That's it for today, Biney. I'll see you in a few days when the hearing aid arrives."

"Thank you," Biney said, as she and her mother left Mr. Wade's office.

4

As Biney and her mother drove home, Biney turned in her seat to see her mother's lips. "Mom, what did Mr. Wade say to you?" she asked.

Surprised, her mother glanced at her. "He thought the hearing aid would help you. Why?"

"I hate it when I'm left out. I hate it." Biney shouted.

"Biney! Look out!"

Biney turned around to look out of the car window. She flinched when she saw a car charging toward them. At the same time, her mother slammed on the brakes. Biney fell forward, bumping her head on the dashboard.

Biney woke up slowly and realized she still was in the car. Strangers were helping her out. Standing awkwardly in the street, she looked for her mother. All she could see were strangers.

"Mom?" whimpered Biney, trying to focus on the unfamiliar faces around her. "Mom?"

Biney noticed that a car was smashed against the front wheel of their car and that the metal of both cars was badly dented. Becoming aware of some commotion behind her,

Biney turned around. She saw her mother, being supported by strangers, coming slowly around the back of their car toward her.

"Oh, Mom," cried Biney, becoming alarmed at the cuts on her mother's face.

"I'm all right, Biney," her mother said, hugging her. "Come on," she urged as she led Biney gently toward a poplar tree and helped her down on the soft grass around it. "Wait here. I'll be back soon."

Biney nodded, closing her eyes. The smell of the sweet clover gently enveloped her. Her forehead throbbed. Moving her fingers up to her forehead, she felt a lump the size of a ping pong ball just above her right eye. She opened her eyes and looked at the crowd around the car. The police officer near her mother was pointing to their car's dented front. The other car had a broken light. The driver of that car, who did not seem to be hurt, stood talking to her mother and the police officer. Biney watched the police officer write his report; he nodded his head several times as the women talked to him. At the same time, another police officer was untangling the fenders on both cars.

"Why are Mom and the police taking so long?" Biney wondered. A few minutes later, the strangers standing around them began to leave, and her mother walked toward her.

"All right, Biney. Let's go," she said.

When they were settled in the car, Biney's mother turned around, looked directly at her, and spoke slowly.

"Biney, we are going to our doctor. I think we will be all right, but I want to be sure. Please don't talk to me while I'm driving."

At the doctor's office, Biney remained quiet while the doctor looked at her eye and forehead and then examined her mother. After they both had been examined, she and her mother drove home from the doctor's in silence.

A half hour later, Biney was sitting uncomfortably in the family room with an ice pack on her forehead. Her mother came in, sat in the other rocking chair, and explained everything that had happened. Biney wanted to know everything, but at the same time, she was angry at the helplessness she had felt not only in Mr. Wade's office, but also during the accident and the visit to the doctor's office.

"The doctor said the knot on your forehead will go down, especially after you use the ice pack. He was concerned about the blood in your eye. It will go away with time. We will go back to him next week to make sure it is all right. Right now, you should stay fairly quiet."

"Can I draw at the pond in the morning?" asked Biney. "I need to make more cards for Mrs. Caldwell."

"Yes, that is a good idea," her mother answered. "Pat called a few minutes ago. She wants you to come over Thursday afternoon, instead of today. I told her about the accident and she promised you two will stay quiet. Maria can drive you there.

"Biney," she continued, "When we are in the car, don't ask questions until I stop driving. You blocked my view of the street. We could have had a bad accident. It's not worth that, is it?"

Biney shook her throbbing head slowly. Her stomach felt like it had a heavy rock rolling around in it trying to get out. *"Mom means the accident was my fault,"* Biney said to herself angrily. *"But, I was just trying to understand what was going on. How come I feel so alone and angry. I don't think it's fair that Mom blames me. She was driving. Nobody understands how I feel."* Biney's thoughts were interrupted by her mother's waving hand.

"I know you realize that we have to talk slowly to you. Other people will not take the time; it won't help for you to get angry. You can understand me better by concentrating on my lips. You will be sidetracked when you try to watch more than one person's lips. So, when we are in a group, even if it is in the doctor's office, always remember to wait until we can talk alone.''

"And half of the time get a 'never mind'?'' asked Biney. "Why bother?''

Biney got up from the rocker and left the room. Glancing back, she saw a look of deep pain on her mother's face, but she resisted running back to hug her. Confused, she trudged upstairs, holding the sturdy oak stair rail for support. Her head throbbed; she couldn't wait to lie down.

Resting on her comfortable brass bed, she began to think about the day's events. *"I wish I had more patience, but I can't help it. It doesn't make sense. Mom is trying to help me, but it just makes me frustrated. Every time I see the empty space above the television where the vase was, it reminds me of the 'never mind' I get when I ask what's going on. Why bother? What chance do I ever have of understanding what's going on around me, anyway?"* she mumbled to herself as she drifted off to sleep.

Early the next morning, as the sun began to rise above the horizon in the pinkish-gray eastern sky, Biney sat on the exposed root of the old maple tree. She quickly drew her pictures, hoping to finish before the hot August sun made her hand too sweaty to work.

"So far, so good,'' whispered Biney. "Just one more card to go.'' She drew a tall-stemmed long-leaved cattail plant with its dense brown, sausage-shaped spike. Near it, she drew an outline of the pond and shaded in the shimmering reflection of the water.

As she worked, she thought about Mrs. Nash, her old art teacher. They had taken long walks together, drawing and painting pictures at the pond, in the woods around the house, on the cliff, and even in the mountains. But Mrs. Nash was now in California working for an advertising agency. Mrs. Nash and Mrs. Caldwell, the stationery store manager, were good friends. Both of them had encouraged Biney to draw.

While Biney was sketching the card, a red-winged blackbird flew to the tip of one of the cattails. The bird's beak opened and closed, and Biney wished she could hear it singing. She quickly sketched the bird next to the cattail. After drawing the head and beak, she grabbed the artgum eraser, rubbing out the too fat body, and redrew a smaller one. Her pencil rapidly outlined a tail, but she had trouble getting it the way she wanted it, so she used the eraser again and again.

"What's the matter with that tail?" she blurted out. Just then, the blackbird flew away toward the cliff as if it had been startled. Sensing that something was wrong, Biney scrutinized the pond. The little inch-long spring peeper frogs jumped from the tangled grass into the water, one right after the other. *"What's bothering them?"* she wondered. Her neck began to tingle and goose pimples rippled up her back. Her eyes searched the grass at the edge of the pond looking for a moving object, like a snake. Then she looked west toward the hill leading to her house. Nothing.

Still feeling uneasy, Biney tried to get back to her drawing. A strong fish smell enveloped the area. Jumping up, she looked in back of her toward the trail that led to the cliff and the river. Her mouth gaped as she caught her breath.

Gene stood behind her, near a small black oak tree. He was close enough to look over her shoulder at the drawing. His fishing pole was leaning against the tree, and two large bass flopped on the ground.

"Hi, dummy," Gene said deliberately. "That's a stupid tail. Why don't you give up?" Then he stared at her. "Oh, look at the black eye! Who did you fight with? Huh? Huh?" he asked, grinning.

Biney watched Gene jump around, acting as if he were boxing. He flexed his muscular arms and clenched his fists in front of his chest. "Pow, pow! Uh, oh; wow, ha ha. Come on, dummy, let's fight."

Biney stood, hands on her hips, feeling her throat tighten at the mention of her black eye. Gene stopped his shadowboxing and looked at Biney. "Geez, can't you take a joke?" he asked.

"Go, go, go!" snapped Biney, glaring at her tormentor. She quickly turned her back to him to avoid seeing his lips, picked up her drawings, and placed the pencils and eraser in the knothole of the maple tree. Feeling a tap on her shoulder, Biney whipped around and pushed his hand away.

"Go away! I don't want to hear 'dummy' again. Go!" she shouted, and immediately turned back to the knothole. A few seconds later, she glanced sideways and saw him walking down the trail, carrying the fish.

Every time Biney saw Gene, her heart started pounding. She knew she wasn't afraid of him, so why did he make her heart jump? Sitting on the tree root and leaning against the trunk, she tried to analyze the situation. *"Gene is really hateful,"* she decided. *"And Pat is so bubbly and so much fun to be with. How could Gene and Pat be so different? Pat's always boasting about how smart Gene is in school and how good he is with computers. He is even good-looking. I just don't understand why he is so mean to me."*

"And why does he call me 'dummy?'" she asked aloud. Then remembering his 'Why don't you give up?', she exclaimed, "No way, I'll never quit."

Biney reached in the knothole and took out her pencils.

33

The bird was gone, but its shape was still in her mind. She struggled with the outline of the tail and gradually drew one that was in the right proportion to the bird's body. Then, she decided to ink in the drawings at home before anything else could happen to them.

Biney put the pencils back in the knothole and scrambled up the hill, past the cedar and oak trees, to the house. Once inside the house, she stood under the cooling breeze of the ceiling fan in the hall, still fussing about Gene. "He better not be there when I go to Pat's house," she announced to the walls.

5

In the early afternoon, Maria drove Biney to Pat's house. "You have Pat call me when you're ready to come home," said Maria.

Biney nodded.

Even though all the houses in the row looked alike, Biney always recognized Pat's by its peeling barn-red front door. When Pat opened the door, Biney waved to Maria and entered the small, hot living room. "Where's Gene?" asked Biney.

"He's gone to a baseball game," answered Pat. "Why?"

"He was at the pond this morning," answered Biney. "I thought maybe he was still here."

"No, he left right after lunch," said Pat. "Mom and Dad are at work, too. Come on, let's cut your hair."

As they walked across the living room, Biney could feel vibrations coming through her sandals. She realized that the television was turned on loud. Pat turned it off.

"What were you watching?" Biney asked, glancing above the television at a framed magazine picture of a boy playing the mandolin.

"There was a special program on bluegrass music," answered Pat, moving her hands as if playing a guitar. "Come on. Let's go to my room."

Biney followed Pat down the short hall to her bedroom. It was just big enough for a single bed and small dresser. A framed mirror hung above the dresser. Biney sat on a chair in front of the dresser, and Pat draped a towel around her shoulders.

"Biney, can you read my lips okay in the mirror?" Pat inquired.

"Yes, as long as you talk slowly," answered Biney.

"You wanted your hair short, right?"

"Yes," said Biney. "But leave it long enough to cover my ears when I have to wear a hearing aid. I don't want anyone to see it."

"Tell me about the hearing test and your black eye," said Pat.

While Biney described Mr. Wade and the car accident, her mind wandered back to the pond and puzzled over Gene's words. She didn't realize it, but she had stopped talking. A sudden yank on her hair brought her back to reality. "Ouch," she cried.

"Oh, sorry, I didn't mean to pull so hard," said Pat, examining Biney's hair in the mirror.

"That's okay," said Biney. "You know, sometimes in school, I can't understand the other kids at all, especially when they are in groups. One time last year a group of kids were talking in the hall and some of them stared at me. I know they were talking about me."

"Why would the kids in school want to talk about you?" asked Pat. "Maybe they were talking about classes or the teachers and just happened to look in your direction. Just because they were looking at you doesn't mean they were talking about you."

Hesitating a second, Pat continued. "Biney, when you were talking before, you stopped several times, as if you wanted to tell me something. Are you afraid to say it? Come on, let's have it. What's on your mind?" Pat continued to cut Biney's hair.

Biney stared at her dark golden hair lying on the floor. "It's Gene," answered Biney. "He always calls me dummy. I hate it. I feel helpless. Will other kids act like Gene in high school? I don't want to go if they do."

Pat reached for a chair and sat down across from Biney.

"Biney," said Pat slowly, peering at Biney as closely as her thick lenses allowed. "You used to be fun to play with. You even laughed at your own hearing mistakes. Why take it so hard now? Maybe…maybe Gene likes you—just a little bit? Some boys act silly when they like a girl. They can't help it. Did you know kids call him Mickey Mouse?"

"No. Why?"

"Because of his big ears. But, he laughs with them and wriggles his ears." Pat pulled on her ears, moving her fingers up and down.

Biney grinned. Wriggle his ears? She tried to move hers while Pat finished cutting her hair.

After what seemed like a few minutes, Pat asked Biney how she liked her hair. Surprised, Biney looked in the mirror. She had been concentrating so closely on Pat's lips that she hadn't paid attention to what Pat was doing to her hair. Somehow, her thin face looked fuller now. Even the freckles on the bridge of her nose didn't stand out as much. Her hair seemed to have a golden shine, and the heart-shaped dip where her hairline met her forehead was gone because she now had bangs.

Biney took a small mirror from the dresser, turned around, and looked at the sides and back of her hair in the larger dresser mirror. Each side feathered toward the back, partly covering her ears. Pat had cut the back in different layers, and the whole back waved a little.

"I love it," Biney exclaimed. "Thanks, Pat. Thanks a lot," she said, hugging Pat.

"Oh, you're welcome," Pat replied. "I loved doing it."

Biney looked at her watch and was surprised at the time. "I better get going, Pat. But, don't call Maria; I want to walk home."

"But Maria told you to have me call her," Pat protested. "Besides, it's an awfully long walk."

"That's okay," Biney responded. "I feel like doing it." Before Pat could argue any more, Biney went to the door. "Bye now, and thanks again."

"Be careful," said Pat. "You have to walk through the bad section of town."

"Oh yeah," Biney reminded herself as she walked down the street. *"I had forgotten about that part of town; the houses are really run-down. Maybe I should have let Pat call Maria. No, no, I have to show everyone I can be independent,"* she decided.

As Biney walked toward the old neighborhood, she told herself that there were only two long blocks and nothing was going to happen in broad daylight. She glanced at the row of tiny unpainted porches. Women, young and old, in faded dresses, many holding little children, sat talking to each other on the porches. Biney saw a fat woman sitting on a flimsy looking chair on the lawn. Biney grinned, thinking what it would look like to see her plop to the ground. The woman grinned back.

Further down the block, Biney watched several young men crowded around a badly dented, dull green car yelling at the couple sitting in it. A few turned to stare at Biney, which made her quicken her pace. Several boys playing baseball in an empty lot covered with empty bottles and candy wrappers stopped playing to watch her walk by.

Puzzled and feeling her neck become taut with fear, Biney walked faster. Looking back toward the fat lady sitting on the flimsy chair, she suddenly found herself tossed to the ground. Her head hit the edge of the sidewalk and her legs became tangled up with another pair of legs and bicycle wheels.

Thoroughly frightened, Biney pushed her hands against the sidewalk to sit up. She felt the hands of several bystanders grab her to help her up. The fat lady ran to the boy who had run into Biney with his bicycle. She spanked him until her hand turned red. A little girl moved the bicycle out of Biney's way.

Biney figured the boy hadn't been looking where he was going. And since she certainly hadn't been watching where she was going, either, she didn't feel he should receive such a hard spanking. She wasn't hurt, just startled.

The boy's mother came over to Biney, talking as she walked. She attempted to get Biney to sit in her flimsy chair. Even though Biney understood only half of what she said, she felt the lady was trying to help her.

"I'm all right. Don't spank him. It wasn't all his fault—I wasn't watching where I was going. I've got to go now. Thanks for your help," she explained to the woman as she pulled away.

Biney continued on her way. She watched for cars as she crossed the busy highway. When she reached the swinging bridge in the public park, she saw some children jumping up and down on the bridge. They were laughing.

"Hi," said Biney. She started jumping, too, making the bridge rock even more.

"Hi," they answered, laughing. Then followed a stream of words.

39

Biney couldn't understand them, but she didn't care, she enjoyed watching their happy faces. She still felt a bit shaky from her walk through the old neighborhood. That boy had been spanked really hard!

The shallow stream under the bridge rippled against rocks and dead branches as it continued on its way. Biney followed the stream for a while until she reached the forked trail near the bluff. She decided to climb to the top instead of walking in front of it. At the top, she paused to catch her breath in the cooling shade of the old trees. The gentle breeze felt good against her flushed face.

From the top of the cliff, Biney looked down at the trail she had just been on and the stream that separated the public park from her house. The highest branches of the trees growing by the stream just reached the top of the cliff. A small ledge halfway down the steep incline was the only break in the drop to the bottom.

Looking among the tree tops, past the pond that she could not see but knew was there, she glanced at the tall house on the hill. She could see the afternoon sun reflecting off her bedroom window, inviting her to hurry safely home. She turned around and began the last leg of her walk home. On the way, she picked up a couple of small oak branches and acorns to take home. She also broke off a leaf from a spicebush with bright red berries and deeply inhaled the tantalizing spicy smell. She remembered how, as a little girl, she and her grandmother had drunk tea, brewed from these leaves.

Walking from the park to a private trail, Biney headed for the pond. With a sigh of relief, she sat on her favorite tree root and leaned against the trunk. She wondered whether she should tell Maria or her mother what had happened? She knew she could have taken a longer way home instead of going through that part of town. She felt her chest tighten as she thought of the people staring at her and the feel of . . . of . . . what? Danger? Not danger. Whatever it was, she didn't want to walk through there anymore.

Leaving the maple tree, she followed the trail up the hill toward home. She opened one of the double doors and peeked in the hall.

"Biney Richmond," Maria scolded as soon as Biney stepped into the cool hall. "I told you to have Pat call me when you were ready to come home."

"I wanted to walk home," Biney declared, with as much confidence as she could. "Besides, Maria, I am old enough to walk home alone."

"Biney," said Maria. "You can't hear the cars on the highway. And what would you do if you got lost? What could I say to your parents if something happened to you?"

"Maria!" exclaimed Biney. "Quit treating me like a little kid. I have brains, don't I? I can see the cars, can't I? I'm going to do what I please, and you and my parents better get used to it!" She turned to the curved oak stairs to avoid looking at Maria's lips.

Maria grabbed Biney's arm and spun her around. "Look, you are not ready for this much freedom. Remember the library? You couldn't understand the librarian. What would you do if a man grabbed you on the sidewalk?"

"I'd run," answered Biney.

"Yeah, sure," Maria snapped. "Look, your mother just drove her car in the driveway. You're going to have a lot of explaining to do before I leave."

"There's another car," Biney observed. "Mom must be bringing someone here. Don't mention my walking home in front of anyone. Please!"

After the two women entered the hall, Maria talked briefly to Biney's mother, then left.

"Biney, please come into the living room with us," her

41

mother requested. Biney loved the airy, pale yellow room. She sat in the rocking chair in front of the sheer window curtains. Her mother and the other woman sat on the sofa facing the rocking chair. From here, Biney could see their lips clearly.

"This is Mrs. Miller, a counselor at the high school," Biney's mom explained to her.

"Biney," said Mrs. Miller slowly, "I wanted to get acquainted with you before school starts."

"While you two talk, I'll make some coffee," Biney's mother interjected.

"Do any of your friends have trouble understanding you?" asked Mrs. Miller.

"No," Biney answered. "But some kids at school can't understand me very well."

"You seem to understand what I say."

"Just a few words. I guess at the rest," Biney replied. "Sometimes only one word mixes me up and usually it's the first word in a sentence. Some kids have to repeat themselves three or four times before I understand them. The *s, ch*, and *sh* give me lots of trouble. So do words that look alike; you know, like *need, jean,* and *clean.*"

"Do you have any friends at school you can go to for help, if necessary?" asked Mrs. Miller.

"Yes, Pat Sullivan," answered Biney. "She'll be in the ninth grade, too. I can understand her pretty well."

"If I write a couple of sentences on a piece of paper, will you read them to me?" asked Mrs. Miller.

Biney nodded. Mrs. Miller wrote down some words and handed the paper to Biney. Biney struggled to pronounce the words clearly:

> How much wood would a woodchuck chuck,
> if a woodchuck could chuck wood.

> The bright sun shone through the church windows, casting shadows on the walls and chairs.

With Mrs. Miller's help, Biney said all the words correctly. Even though she seemed to say the words properly, she still couldn't tell the difference between the *sh* and *ch* sounds.

"Now say them fast, especially the first one," Mrs. Miller requested.

Biney's lips puckered as she stumbled and laughed over the phrases.

"In one of your classes, you will spend some time working on the sounds that you have trouble with," continued Mrs. Miller.

Biney's mother returned with the coffee and some lemonade for Biney.

"Thank you, Mrs. Richmond," said the counselor. "You know, Biney speechreads very well."

"Thank you. Please call me Nanette. Biney's name is really Binette, which is a combination of my husband's name, Bill, and my name. Of course, everyone calls her Biney now."

"It's very unusual," Mrs. Miller observed.

"Biney, do you have any questions about school?"

"Do the teachers know I'm deaf?" asked Biney.

"Not yet," said Mrs. Miller. "When you get your schedule and find out who your teachers are, we will talk with them. I have an office at school; you can come see me when you have problems. I can also arrange for someone to take notes for you, if you want. You think about it and let me know once your classes start." She finished her coffee and stood up to leave. "Well, I must go. See you soon, Biney."

After Mrs. Miller left, Biney helped her mother carry the dishes into the kitchen. Her mother looked at her for a minute with a puzzled expression and then said, "I like your hair very much. But I wish you had told me you wanted to cut it. I could have made an appointment for you with my hairdresser."

"That's okay, Mom," Biney replied. "Pat did it for me; I wanted to surprise everyone. Don't say anything to Dad. Let's see if he notices it when he gets home from his trip."

"That's fine with me," answered Mom, walking toward the refrigerator. "It's time to prepare dinner. I could use some help. We will eat in the kitchen since Daddy won't be home. You can set the table for me."

Biney piled the plates, cups, and silverware on a tray. She was about to take everything over to the table when she felt her mother's hand on her shoulder. Looking at her mother's lips, she recognized her firm, angry expression.

"Biney, what's this about you walking home by yourself?"

Biney's mouth fell open in disbelief. *"Why did Maria have to tell Mom I walked home?"* She looked at her mother for a long moment, trying to decide what to say.

"Mom, I'm tired of not being trusted. You act as if I can't think just because I can't hear. Come on, Mom, I've got a brain. I'm almost fourteen years old. I'm old enough to do things by myself."

Picking up the tray of dishes from the counter she took the few steps to the table in the kitchen nook and slammed the tray down on the red and white checked tablecloth. She fought back tears as she slumped on the built-in bench behind the table. Bringing her feet up on the cushion, she leaned against the wide window frame, wrapped her arms around her knees, and stared, unseeing, at the cardinals and sparrows under the trees.

Biney's mother walked over and put her hand on Biney's shoulder. Biney looked up at her mother.

"If you go places by yourself and need help, you'll have to explain that you're deaf."

"Mom, I won't need help," Biney declared. "I can do things on my own. I won't have you or Maria with me all my life, you know. I have to start doing things without you."

"All right," said her mom, giving in. "I'll tell Maria, but you must let us know where you are and when to expect you back. I don't think you realize the problems you'll run into."

Biney stared at her mother's quivering lips. *"Is Mom afraid?"* she wondered. Getting up from the bench, she stood before her mother, frowning. "Mom, please quit worrying about me," she hollered.

"All right, Biney. Stop yelling. The phone is ringing."

She returned a few minutes later. "That was Mr. Wade. Your hearing aid is ready. We can go get it now."

6

Biney sat in Mr. Wade's office watching him connect the parts of the hearing aid. Speaking slowly, he explained where the battery went and how to insert it in the hearing aid. Then he placed the earmold in her ear and adjusted the dial. All the while he kept talking. He turned away from Biney, still talking into the hearing aid. Turning back, he faced her and asked, "Could you hear me?"

"Yes, but I didn't understand you."

"That takes time. You have to learn how to use the hearing aid. This aid will help you hear sounds around you, including speech. With practice, you will be able to recognize some words," Mr. Wade assured her. "When you are home, adjust the volume dial until you are comfortable with the sounds you hear."

"There's one thing you have to remember, Biney. The hearing aid makes all sounds louder. It won't make one sound clearer than another. That's why you have to find a volume that's comfortable for you."

When Biney and her mother arrived home, they sat down in the family room to test the new hearing aid. Allen watched from his dad's easy chair. Biney thought the ear-mold felt funny in her ear; she wondered if she'd ever get used to it. She also hoped that no one could see the hearing aid behind her ear. While her mother talked to her, Biney turned the volume dial until her mother's voice sounded pleasant to her ear.

"Can you hear me?" her mom asked. "What does my voice sound like?"

"It's pretty, Mom," Biney responded, surprised to find that her own voice sounded strange.

"What about me?" asked Allen.

"Loud and clear;" said Biney, "that is, as long as I can see your lips. What have you been doing?"

"Playing with Jim," answered Allen slowly. "We had our cars all over his backyard."

"Biney," said her mom. "The clock is about ready to strike. Do you want to hear it?"

"Yes, yes," Biney exclaimed, running to the clock in the hall. At the same time, she turned the volume in her hearing aid way up because she was afraid she would not be able to hear it. Then she placed her hands expectantly on the walnut body of the clock to feel its vibration.

Bong.

With the first bong, she recoiled at the unexpected loudness. She quickly turned down the volume of the hearing aid and was awed by the clock's beautiful tones.

Bong, bong, bong, bong.

"Wow, oh wow," whispered Biney. "Oh wow-w-w."

For the next hour, Biney and Allen explored various rooms in the house while their mother prepared dinner. Allen played the piano so Biney could hear its sound. He played one key at a time up the scale, and she discovered that each one had a different sound. She even heard one key that didn't sound like it belonged with the others.

"Allen, how come that key plays lower than all the rest?" Biney asked.

Allen quickly played the keys in order. "It doesn't," he answered.

"Yes, it does," Biney insisted.

"Maybe you can't hear that one," said Allen.

"Oh," said Biney. "I guess that means I won't hear music like you do."

"But at least you can hear some music, can't you?" asked Allen.

"Children, children, go wash your hands," their mother called. "Let's eat."

Biney and Allen raced to the bathroom near the kitchen. Allen turned the faucet on all the way, sending water everywhere. Biney closed her eyes and listened to the rushing sound. She jumped, startled to feel cold water running down her arms and legs.

"Uh, oh; look who wet her pants," Allen giggled.

"I'm going to get you for this," Biney warned, grabbing a towel and whipping it against Allen's legs. "I hope this hurts."

"Hey! What's going on here?" said a loud voice.

Startled, Biney and Allen stopped playing.

"Daddy. Daddy. I heard your voice." Biney shouted excitedly.

"I'm glad, Biney," he replied. "Now both of you clean up this mess before I get angry. No more splashing water, Allen.

"Mom told me you got your hearing aid, Biney. The water could ruin it. Have either of you thought of that?"

Biney and Allen shook their heads.

"I'm sorry Dad," said Allen. "You okay, Biney?"

"Yeah, I'm fine," she answered.

"I finished my job earlier than expected and I'm

hungry," continued Dad. "Clean up the bathroom and then let's eat."

"Biney," Maria said the next morning, "your mother told me you can walk to town by yourself. But I need to get some supplies. So why don't I drive you there and you can walk back home."

"Okay," Biney agreed. "I need to go to the library."

After returning the books to the library, Biney walked down the town's main street and looked in all the store windows.

In the window of an antique store, she spotted a vase that looked almost exactly like the one she had broken at home. Standing on tiptoe at the window, she tried to read the price tag that was wrapped around the neck of the vase. Just then a small group of people entered the antique store. Biney walked in as part of the group. Once in the store, she worked her way around the narrow, crowded aisles to the vase. Biney looked at the tag and realized she didn't have enough money to buy it.

A spindly old woman moved toward Biney, talking in a scratchy voice. She appeared to be gritting her teeth—and still talking. The woman kept looking at Biney's ear.

Biney became uneasy. The woman didn't appear very friendly.

"Save that vase for me, please," Biney requested, not knowing if the woman understood her.

Turning around to leave, she noticed an antique mirror and looked at her ear. Even though the hearing aid was partly covered by her short hair, she felt it was noticeable. She was sure that was why the store owner was staring at her.

The woman worked her way through the antiques and

grabbed Biney's arm. She guided her firmly toward the door and into the dry heat of late summer.

Going to the window again to look at the vase, Biney noticed a large sign above a table piled high with glass dishes.

BREAK A DISH—YOU PAY FOR IT
NO CHILDREN ALLOWED

"No children, huh," she thought. *"I don't care about you, old woman, I'm going to buy that vase."*

As Biney walked toward the stationery store two more blocks down the main street, she tried to figure out how many cards she would have to paint and sell to buy the vase. If she worked hard, maybe she could get enough done in three or four days. That would give her enough money to pay off some of the layaway on her new outfit and buy the vase.

When she reached the stationery store, Biney found Mrs. Caldwell. She pointed to her hearing aid.

"Why, Biney," Mrs. Caldwell exclaimed. "That's wonderful. What does my voice sound like to you?"

"It's deep," answered Biney. "You sound like you're singing. I still have to watch your lips, though."

"Yes, of course," said Mrs. Caldwell. "But at least you can hear some things."

"Here are some more of the pictures," said Biney. "I didn't get as many done this time."

"They are beautiful! Do as many more as you can. Wait. Before you go, let me pay you for the work you've finished."

After she left the stationery store, Biney began to walk home. She passed the drugstore where she and Maria often stopped for milk shakes. One of their friends was a waitress in the coffee shop. Impulsively, Biney decided to get a milk shake. She knew she could do it by herself, even though she had never ordered one before. Maria had always done it.

Pushing the massive door open, Biney walked down the aisle toward the booth at the back where she and Maria usually sat. She noticed a group of boys staring at her from a nearby booth and she began to feel nervous. A strange waitress headed toward her. Surprised at not seeing her old friend, Biney waited quietly as the waitress put a glass of water and paper napkin on the table. She stared at the waitress's mouth. Her lips stretched over her big teeth, almost like the lips of a monkey Biney had seen last year at the zoo.

"Chocolate shake, please," Biney ordered, smiling. She quickly banished the thought of the monkey.

The waitress did not move. She continued talking and looking at Biney. Concentrating harder, Biney stared closely at the flopping lips, trying to understand the words they were forming. There was too much other noise in the drugstore for Biney to hear well, so she turned her hearing aid down. Thinking the waitress had not understood her, Biney repeated her request.

"Chocolate shake, please."

The waitress stopped talking and stared at her, pencil poised over the order pad. What was wrong? Fiddling with the glass of water, she stared at the waitress's lips, watching and waiting.

The waitress remained still, staring at Biney.

"Forget it," Biney blurted. She rushed out of the drugstore, fighting the tears that threatened to escape from her eyes. *"Why didn't the waitress understand me?"* she asked herself. *"I spoke slowly. I thought my words were clear enough for the waitress to understand. What was the problem? And this hearing aid didn't help at all. I could only hear a lot of noise.''* A tap on her shoulder startled her to an abrupt halt.

A muscular, blond, teenage boy stood before her. Biney recognized him as one of the group of boys in the drugstore.

"My name is Carl," he said slowly. "Are you Biney?" She nodded.

"Pat and Gene are my friends," he explained. "Are you okay? That waitress asked if you wanted a large or small shake." He moved his hands up and down to indicate the size. "Come on, let's go back. I'll help you get it."

Biney vigorously shook her head no and walked on to keep Carl from seeing the tears streaming down her cheeks. Feeling a tap on her shoulder again, she turned around. A drugstore paper napkin dangled in front of her eyes. When it was lowered, she saw Carl's impish grin.

"Let me walk you home," Carl suggested.

Wiping her tears with the napkin, Biney nodded hesitantly. Moving her eyes constantly—from the sidewalk to keep track of where she was walking to Carl's lips to see what he was saying—Biney listened closely to the faint sound of Carl's voice.

While they were walking, a rescue squad van came roaring down the street. Biney covered her ears against the piercing sound of the siren. "Owww," she cried. "That sure is loud."

"Come on, Biney," Carl said, grabbing Biney's hand. They hurried across the highway. Carl held onto Biney's hand as they walked to the swinging bridge. They followed the trail to the foot of the cliff, where they found a shallow cave. It was dark and cool inside. When they left the cave, Biney and Carl took the path to the private trail leading to Biney's favorite tree. They sat down on the root to rest.

"Biney, don't let what happened at the drugstore bother you," Carl advised. "You will go back, won't you?"

"Right now, no," answered Biney.

"Why?" asked Carl. "You can tell the waitress you can't hear well and that she needs to talk more slowly."

"I don't want her to know I can't hear well," Biney replied.

"Why? It really bothers you, doesn't it?"

Biney nodded.

"Look, Pat can't see well," continued Carl. "You can't hear well. Pat wears glasses. You have a hearing aid. What's the difference? You can't stay home all your life. Come on, please try again."

"Maybe . . . someday," she mumbled reluctantly, her voice shaking.

"Don't wait too long," Carl urged.

"This is where I usually come to draw for Mrs. Caldwell," Biney announced in an effort to change the conversation. "I make note cards, and she sells them in her store."

"That's great! Can I see some of your drawings?" Carl said.

"I have a few in my art room," answered Biney. "Come on, I'll show them to you."

While walking uphill toward the house, Biney wondered how Maria was going to react to her new friend. *"What kind of explanation should I give her about the drugstore? Why even bother mentioning it,"* she decided.

Maria was sitting on the front porch when they reached Biney's house. "Maria, this is Carl," said Biney, "He knows Pat and Gene, and he helped me across the highway."

"Hello, Carl," said Maria. "Thanks for the help."

"Carl wants to see my drawings," Biney explained.

"Sure," said Maria. "I haven't looked at your drawings for a long time either," said Maria. "I'll go, too."

53

Biney, Carl, and Maria filed up the oak stairs and through the upstairs hall to the front of the house. Biney went to a small door at the end of the hall and opened the door into a tiny room that was just big enough for a chair and a small table. The table was covered with art paper, a big jar filled with paint brushes of various sizes, and an old shoe box of tubes of acrylic paints. Biney watched Carl and Maria examine the drawings of flowers, vases, and baskets that were tacked to the walls below the porthole windows.

"Hey, they're good," Carl observed, turning to Biney. "I especially like the drawing of the cattails at the pond."

Biney opened another door leading to a tiny balcony that provided shade to the L-shaped porch underneath.

"Someday, I want to paint that," said Biney, pointing to the cliff, pond, trees, and stream. "Right now, I don't think I'm ready."

"Are you taking art in school this year?" asked Carl.

"Yes, I am," answered Biney.

"I'm glad," said Maria.

"Can I watch you draw sometime?" asked Carl.

"Okay," said Biney. "I'm at the maple tree most mornings."

Returning downstairs, Maria offered Biney and Carl some lemonade.

"Thanks," said Carl. "I'd like to, but I don't have time. I have to go now. See you later."

"Well," said Maria, turning to Biney. "How do you like having a boyfriend?"

"You think he's cute?" asked Biney.

"Yeah, I do," Maria replied. "Biney, I don't mean to change the subject, but why don't you try calling Pat on the phone. Ask her over for your birthday on Tuesday."

"All right. Let me dial," said Biney.

"After you dial, let me listen to make sure we get Pat," Maria suggested.

Biney adjusted her hearing aid to the telephone switch, dialed, and waited impatiently.

"Okay, Biney, Pat is on the phone."

"Hi, Pat," said Biney. "Can you come over for cake and ice cream Tuesday?" She waited, then, hearing a garbled sound, she listened more closely.

"What did she say?" asked Maria.

"I think she said yes."

"Here, let me talk to her," said Maria, grabbing the receiver.

Biney frowned as she stood by Maria, waiting. *"Maria can talk to Pat anytime. Maria's voice is beautiful and her words are so distinct. My voice sounds harsh. I couldn't even recognize some of the words myself,"* she complained. *"Why did I get this hearing aid anyway?"*

"Pat can come," said Maria as she replaced the receiver. "You know, I think we ought to invite Gene and Carl, too."

"No, you don't," protested Biney. "No you don't. You can ask Jim for Allen to play with, but that's all."

Maria stood in front of Biney, grinning.

Biney caught the look. "Oh you," she said, angry at first, then she slowly grinned back at Maria.

"Biney, you shouldn't take things so seriously," Maria suggested.

7

On Saturday morning, Carl was waiting when Biney reached the pond. He watched as she sketched the cliff behind the pond. Later, Biney watched Carl explore the pond. First, he dipped a small jar into the water, then he came back to the maple tree and took out a slide and hand lens from his duffel bag.

"Look at the slide, Biney. You have to look closely to see the cyclops. Their bodies are transparent. They are food for the fish."

Biney placed the pencils back into the knothole of the maple tree and went over to examine the moving specks in the jar. The hand lens made the specks appear somewhat bigger. By concentrating on one specimen, she discovered the body appeared to be segmented and the tail, also segmented, forked at the tip. The cyclops moved in jerks; its long antennae felt its surroundings as it skimmed through the water. Biney was fascinated with its single eye.

"Hey, they're pretty," exclaimed Biney. "How did you know they were in the pond water?"

"My dad gave me a microscope for my birthday last

year and ever since, I have been looking at them. You know, these cyclops belong to the same group as the crabs, shrimps, pillbugs, and lobsters,'' Carl told her. ''They have a hard outer cover on the body like a crayfish.''

Biney looked puzzled, so Carl repeated what he had said.

''Neat,'' said Biney.

''Yeah,'' Carl agreed, as he packed up his things. ''I gotta go now, Biney. Is it okay if I come back again sometime?''

''Sure,'' Biney answered grinning. ''See you soon,'' she called as he walked away.

Arriving at the maple tree the next morning, Biney stared, surprised, at the piece of white paper folded in the knothole. She took out the note, unfolded it carefully, and read the penciled words. She stared at them in disbelief. She looked around to see if anyone was watching her, then read the words again: ''You're cute.''

Again, Biney looked among the trees, especially toward the cliff, but saw no sign of anyone.

Carl did not come to the pond that day. The next morning, Biney found another note. It said, ''I like the freckles on your nose.''

''Ugh,'' Biney groaned. ''How can anyone stand those freckles? I wonder who's writing these notes? It's probably Carl,'' she thought out loud. ''But it could be Allen. Maybe he meant them to be a birthday present.''

Biney examined the note again. The f in freckles was written with a backward bottom loop. Although she felt sure Allen didn't write like that, she decided to look at some of his school notes from last spring.

Biney walked into her house as quietly as she could. She saw that Maria was busy in the kitchen, so she went quickly upstairs into Allen's room. The curtains, which Allen had picked out especially because they showed different types of antique cars, were swaying back and forth in the breeze.

Biney pushed aside the curtains and looked out. She saw Allen and Jim playing with their model cars, driving them around and under the tree roots near the creek. She looked beyond the rippling water to the shopping mall and the condominium where Maria lived with her parents.

Among the toys and books in the bookcase near Allen's bunk bed was a box that had not been touched since school let out last spring. Biney opened the box, picked out a few of Allen's class papers, and scanned the words to find the letter *f*. *"There it is,"* said Biney to herself. *"Well, it wasn't Allen who wrote the notes,"* she concluded.

Replacing the papers in the box, she left Allen's room and followed the wide upstairs hall to the art room. As she inked in the cliff drawing, she compared Gene to Carl. *"It makes me really angry,"* she admitted to herself, *"when Gene calls me a dummy or makes fun of my drawings. But Carl likes my paintings. I wonder if Gene means what he says?"* Then she remembered what Pat said.

"Some boys act silly. They can't help it."

"Maybe that's it," she thought. *"So why should I be upset by his actions? When Carl held my hand, I was surprised and excited and not certain whether I liked it. He kept showing me things at the pond that I never thought to examine, and he spent time teaching me about them. He didn't seem to mind repeating the words until I understood them, either. Gene would never do that."*

After looking at the two notes for the dozenth time, Biney slipped them between the bottom lid of the paint box and the box itself. She was so absorbed in her thoughts about the boys that her heart jumped when she felt a tap on her shoulder. She looked up, obviously surprised to see Maria standing there.

"Your dad wants to talk to you on the phone," Maria said.

Biney ran to the downstairs hall telephone, relieved that Maria had not seen her put the notes under the box.

"Hi, Dad."

"Hi! I . . . home . . . er . . . day."

"Dad, I can't understand you," Biney said. "What did you say?" She recognized the sounds were being repeated.

"I . . . home . . . er . . . day," her dad said again.

"Dad, I'm turning the phone over to Maria," she said. "I really can't understand you."

Maria listened, then returned the receiver to Biney. "He wants you to keep listening to him," Maria told her. "See if you can't recognize some of the words."

Biney closed her eyes and concentrated on the words. She moved her lips to form the sounds she thought she heard.

"I . . . for . . . day."

"Dad, the only words I understood were I, for, and day," Biney complained. "Are you coming home for my birthday?"

"Yes, I am," he answered.

Handing the phone back to Maria, she sat down, feeling weak. She was sure she was not going to feel comfortable with the telephone—ever.

Biney woke up early Tuesday morning. She stretched and relaxed between her pale yellow sheets. *"Fourteen years old! Now I'm as old as Pat, at least for six months, anyway,"* she told herself proudly. *"I'm wide awake. What should I do? Pat won't be over until this afternoon, and it's too early for the rest of the family to be awake. I might as well draw another set of cards,"* she decided.

"I wonder if there's a note in the tree?" Biney whispered to herself.

Hoping there would be one, she jumped out of bed and grabbed a pair of pale green shorts and a cream knit shirt from her wardrobe. She dressed quickly and went into her art room to get her drawing supplies. She tiptoed down the stairs and opened one of the double doors as quietly as she could.

Biney walked across the porch toward the hill leading down to the pond. She stood on the hill for a few minutes letting the cool misty air coat her like a deep moisturizing lotion. While she watched, the fog gradually disappeared as the sun rose above the horizon.

Biney took a deep breath of the spicy smell of the red cedar trees and began walking down the hill. Her feet tingled pleasantly in the dew-filled grass. Halfway down to the old maple tree, she discovered a black and yellow spider sitting in the middle of its perfectly formed web. The web, hanging between two cedar trees, shone in the early morning sunlight. Drops of dew hung precariously from each sparkling strand. When Biney touched the web with her pencil, the spider darted toward it. She jerked her hand back.

"A drawing of the web would be perfect for my cards," she thought. She was afraid the dew would disappear with the approaching warmth from the sun, so she anxiously began drawing. But was there a note in the maple tree? *"The note will keep, but the dew will not,"* she told herself. She began drawing with a sense of urgency. In the back of her mind was the tantalizing thought that a note might be waiting in the tree hole.

After penciling the outline of the web, Biney attempted to add the sparkling dew. The more she tried to work with the dew drops, the more they looked like flat dull buttons hanging from the web. After trying for an hour, she threw the art supplies on the grass in frustration. She studied the drawing, trying to think of a way to make the dew sparkle. Suddenly remembering the note, she ran down the hill toward the maple tree and peeked into the hole.

There was no note.

Crestfallen, Biney stood still and stared at the hole. Then slowly she returned to her drawing. By the time she got back to the web, the dew had disappeared and she had lost her desire to draw. She gathered her art and supplies and returned to the house.

Later that afternoon, Biney sat down in her favorite wicker chair by the bay window in her bedroom and wrote in her diary.

August 27

Dear Diary,

Today is my birthday. I am fourteen. Pat, Jim, and Maria came over this afternoon to share chocolate birthday cake with me. The white frosting was decorated with an art palette that had daubs of different colored frosting that looked like paint. Maria made the cake. It was really good.

I got a lot of nice gifts. One was in a big box, and I saved that one for last. What did I get for my birthday? A book on trees from Maria; candy from Jim; this diary from Pat; a camera from Daddy, a nice one; and a palette from Allen. The big box was from Mom. It contained the shirt and jeans that I wanted so much. I had made a few payments on them. Mom really surprised me by finishing the payments in time for my birthday. Plus, she added another outfit to go along with it. I love them. I love all my gifts.

My aunts and uncles came to wish me a happy birthday. They stayed to visit with Mom and Dad. Aunt Mildred was easy to understand with my hearing aid, but I couldn't understand the others.

I wish I could understand my uncles. They always look like they're having a good time. They tease each other a lot and tell funny stories. I only see them laugh at the results.

Later, as Pat and I were walking down to the old maple tree, we talked about Carl. I told her how I enjoyed being with him. And I told her about the notes I had been getting, up to this morning, that is. Pat was really surprised. She said Gene goes to Carl's house to lift weights. She likes him, too.

When we arrived at the maple tree, we discovered a note and a pretty flower. The note read, "Happy Birthday."

How did Carl know it was my birthday? I asked Pat if she told him. She said no. She hasn't even seen him for a while.

I had a surprise birthday visit from Mrs. Nash, my old art teacher. She brought me a drawing of my favorite TV star. I want to get a frame for that one!

I took her upstairs to my art room and showed her the spider web drawing I had had so much trouble with. She took a paintbrush and dabbed a little white paint on one side of each dew drop. That's all it took to make it look real! Will I ever be able to draw like her?

Everybody's gone now. That's why I have time to write this. I think I like the idea of having a diary. I can write anything. Even my feelings. There's only one catch. Allen is a real snoop, and if I write everything I want to, I'll have to find a good place to hide you. Well, It's almost time for Allen and me to go to the movies. I'm going to wear my new outfit!

Biney closed the diary and got up from the wicker chair. *"Where can I hide it?"* she asked herself. The built-in seat in the bay window was out; it was too easy a place for Allen to get into. She walked toward the wardrobe and studied the drawers on one side and the shelf over the rod. Pulling out the bottom drawer, she noticed that the bottom of the wardrobe was dark. Her book was dark and it blended with the bottom of the wardrobe. *"A perfect place,"* she thought. *"Nobody would think to look under the drawer."* After struggling to replace the drawer, she got ready for the movies. She felt really cool in her new outfit.

Maria dropped Biney and Allen at the movie theater. "Enjoy the movie, and remember to wait for your mother right here," she told them. "I'll see you tomorrow."

Biney walked up to the ticket window. "One adult and one child, please," she said to the cashier, inserting her money through the slotted glass.

When the cashier spoke to her, Biney just nodded, unwilling to ask her what she had said. The cashier gave her two tickets and the change.

Biney gave the money to Allen so he could buy popcorn and drinks.

"Where's the rest of the money?" asked Allen.

"There isn't anymore," she answered. "That's all the cashier gave me."

"Something's wrong," said Allen. "There's not enough here. Go back to the cashier for the right change."

"No!" Biney snapped. She absolutely would not face the cashier.

8

"Gee whiz, do we have to watch the movie without drinks?" asked Allen, as they sat down near the screen. "I'm hungry." After watching the movie for about ten minutes, he turned to Biney again. "I'm thirsty."

Biney ignored him. The movie didn't hold her attention. She couldn't understand very much of the story, even with her hearing aid on. And the background scenery, which she usually enjoyed, wasn't very interesting, especially with Allen fussing at her. She felt miserable.

After the movie, Biney and Allen waited, in silence, for their mother to pick them up.

"We didn't get popcorn or even a drink," Allen reported to his mother as he and Biney got in the car.

"All right, Allen," said Mom. "We'll talk about this at home. Right now, let me drive."

"Another ride in silence," Biney muttered to herself.

When they got home, Biney went into the living room and waited for her parents to come in. They sat down across from her and listened while she described how she had bought the tickets. Her mother got up from the sofa and said, "Wait here, I'm going to call the theater."

Biney fidgeted on the sofa knowing she had made a mistake not asking the cashier to repeat her question. *"Would I have understood the cashier a second time?"* she wondered. *"I doubt it. And I don't think that hearing aid is helping at all."* She waited impatiently for her mother to come back, avoiding looking at her father in the meantime. Biney looked at her mother for signs of anger when she returned.

"Biney, the cashier says she asked you if both of you were over twelve and you nodded yes, so she sold you two adult tickets. If you had bought a child's ticket for Allen, you would have had enough money for food and drinks.

"Biney, when you don't understand what someone says to you, you will have to explain that you are hearing impaired. And, you must ask the person to speak more slowly."

"I don't want to do that!" Biney declared. "Then everybody will know that I can't understand them. I thought the hearing aid was supposed to help me, but it's not. I don't even want to wear it anymore. I don't want anybody to see it."

"If you don't wear it, what's the point in having it?" her father asked. "The hearing aid is supposed to help you understand. You need to wear it every day to get used to different sounds. You haven't given it a chance. I expect you to wear it all the time. Understand?"

Biney nodded, surprised and upset by the look of anger on her dad's face. He so seldom got angry.

As she got ready for bed, Biney became angry at her parents' demands. She didn't feel ready to wear her hearing aid all the time. She didn't see how it helped her when it seemed like she had more problems than ever before. More and more she resented the lump in her ear, sitting there for everyone to see.

Early the next morning, Biney quietly left the house through the back door, carrying her clipboard and pencils. She sat in the chair on the porch. In the backyard, she noticed for the first time that the holly tree, which was almost hidden by the large oak and cedar trees surrounding it, was full with red berries.

Christmas was only four months away. She wanted to begin drawing Christmas scenes on the cards, especially scenes with the holly and the cedar trees. If she painted as many cards as possible today and sold them, she would have enough to buy the vase she saw in the antique shop.

As Biney drew the holly, she went over in her mind what had happened the night before. She was still unwilling to wear her hearing aid. She felt comfortable with the stillness as she sat in the early morning shade. *"What would be the point of wearing the hearing aid now?"* she questioned. "There's nothing going on. Even the birds aren't doing anything."

Taking a break from her drawing, Biney looked more closely around the yard. She saw a blue jay on a high tree branch, moving back and forth as if it were angry. Its beak opened and closed several times. A bright red cardinal flitted around the cedar tree a few times and then flew away. In a short time, he came back with an insect in his beak. Biney could see the mother cardinal on the nest. She also saw sparrows pecking at the ground underneath the tree. *"Besides the birds, I wonder what other sounds are out here?"* she asked herself. Deciding to find out, she went up to her room to get her hearing aid and returned to the porch. She listened carefully as she gradually turned up the volume of the hearing aid.

The blue jay was still acting up. His cry of "thief" was loud and clear, surprising her with its forcefulness. *"All* right," she acknowledged, *"but what else can I hear? Nothing. I thought so."*

Going back to her drawing, Biney concentrated on the holly with the red berries. As she drew, she noticed a faint rustling sound. *"What was that?"* She looked up not knowing what to expect. Turning up the volume in the hearing aid, she turned her head in several different directions trying to locate the sound. She soon discovered that the static of the hearing aid shut out the faint sound. After turning the volume down, she listened to the steady faint rippling sound and realized that, whatever it was, it would continue that way. She decided to finish drawing the cards first and investigate later.

An hour later, Biney was startled by a whirring sound. She discovered that it came from the two cardinals, who were taking turns darting to and from the cedar tree. Their screeching sounded like anger. Biney frowned and wondered what was wrong with them. The birds looked like they were attacking the tree, but why would they attack like that? Looking more closely at the tree, she noticed a black line part way up. The birds were diving toward that black line, pecking at it.

Feeling uneasy, Biney got up from the porch and maneuvered through the other trees toward the cedar so the birds would not notice her. Still at some distance, she stood quietly studying the black line. Inching closer, she discovered the head of a black snake moving around in the cardinal's nest. Quickly searching the ground near her, Biney grabbed a stick and pushed the snake away from the nest.

But she was too late. Biney saw the lump in the snake's neck and no baby birds in the nest. After the snake crawled away, Biney returned to the chair and watched the parent birds.

The cardinals had stopped flying and were settled in a nearby tree. She faintly heard the plaintive call of the parent birds and realized they were calling for a response from the nest. One of the red birds flew to the nest, then returned to the tree. Soon both left.

Tears ran down Biney's cheeks. The screeching and the pitiful calls of the parent birds were the saddest sounds she had ever heard.

"Hey Biney, what are you doing out here?" Allen asked as he came out on the porch.

Biney could not answer for a moment because of the lump in her throat. "Did you hear anything?" she finally asked.

"Yeah, the birds were making a lot of noise," answered Allen. "Even Mom was wondering about it."

"How would you feel if you knew a black snake got the baby birds?"

"Oh," said Allen nodding. "I know it happens. Dad told me to expect that among animals."

"Have you ever listened to birds cry?" Biney inquired. "It's really disturbing."

"Yes, I know it is," Allen agreed. "After a while you sort of get used to the sound. Dad says life goes on. The birds will just start over and make another nest. That's sort of like Dad telling us that when we have problems, we have to work out the solutions."

"Yeah, like my problem at the movie....Allen, what is that low rustling sound?"

Allen sat on the porch steps and listened. "It could be the wind blowing in the trees. It's awfully faint though."

"No, it sounds like it's far away," Biney replied. "I can barely hear it. It is steady, and keeps going on and on."

"Do you mean the river?" asked Allen. "It's not a faint sound for me, but that could be what you hear. Come on, let's find out."

As they walked toward the river, the sound gradually became louder.

"Yes, that's it," Biney shouted excitedly. "It sounds far away, but it's a soothing sound."

Later that afternoon, while sitting in the wicker chair in her room, Biney wrote in her diary about the cardinals' tragic experience. She was so absorbed in her diary that she didn't notice Maria until she felt a tapping on her shoulder.

"Your mother called," Maria informed her. "Your dad is coming home for supper after all. He doesn't have to go away until tomorrow. We don't have time to cook supper so she asked me to get carry-out chicken. You wait here until I get back."

"Wait, Maria. Let me bake the chocolate chip cookies while you're gone. I want to surprise Mom and Dad."

"No, I think I better be here when you bake."

"Oh, come on, please," Biney pleaded. "You know how many times I have done it with you. I can hear the timer now with my hearing aid. Come on. This is my chance to do it all by myself."

Maria hesitated. "Well, all right. Let's go over the recipe."

"All right!" Biney shouted, skipping downstairs toward the kitchen to get the recipe.

After going over the recipe Maria cautioned Biney, "Remember to stay close to the stove so you'll be sure to hear the timer. I'll be back in a little while. Good luck."

Biney eagerly began to make the cookies. She took out all the ingredients and put them on the counter before mixing the batter.

After turning on the oven to 350° she measured 2¼ cups of flour, 1 teaspoon of salt, and 1 teaspoon of baking soda into the flour sifter, sifted them into a bowl, and set the bowl aside. Next, she used the electric mixer to cream together 1 cup of softened butter and 1½ cups of brown sugar. When that mixture was nice and creamy, she stirred in 1½ teaspoons of vanilla, and then she beat in 2 eggs. When she was sure that the eggs were thoroughly mixed in, she turned down the mixing speed and added the flour mixture. Finally, Biney got a big spoon and folded 2 cups of chocolate chips into the batter.

She had to stand on a footstool to get three cookie sheets from the cupboard. She placed them on the counter and greased them well. Then, she used two spoons to drop mounds of the cookie batter about an inch apart on the cookie sheets. She used the rubber spatula to get the last little bit of the batter. Placing the cookie sheets in the oven, she set the oven timer for twelve minutes.

"There," said Biney with pleasure. "This will show them I can do it."

She felt good.

While waiting for the cookies to bake, Biney sat in the breakfast nook and looked out the window. The majestic old trees, planted years ago by her grandparents, provided wonderful shade in the backyard. She felt a sudden urge to draw the big cedar as a Christmas tree, so she checked the oven timer and decided she had plenty of time to get her art supplies.

Biney drew a faint outline of the evergreen tree on one side of the folded card with a pencil. Then, she filled her rapidograph pen and drew the tree, line by line, very carefully so as not to make a mistake. *"There is no way to erase India ink,"* she reminded herself. *"Hmmm, those cookies smell good."*

Choosing a deep green color, she painted the tree, adding a little white for snow. "Now for the second card," she said aloud.

Suddenly she looked up, sniffing hard. "What's that smell? Oh, no, the cookies," she yelled as she ran to the oven.

9

Biney turned the oven off, grabbed a pot holder, opened the oven door, and took out the cookie sheets. She put them on top of the stove. Then she looked at them. The cookies bubbled and popped. The chocolate chips, now burnt, oozed and blended with the blackened cookie dough.

Wailing in anguish, Biney sat down, placed her head in her arms, and sobbed.

Strong arms comforted Biney. She looked up. "Oh, Daddy." Then she started crying all over again.

Her dad gave her a large handkerchief. "Now Biney, it can't be that bad. Want to tell me about it?"

"I wanted to surprise you and Mom," Biney explained. "But, I didn't hear the timer, even though I have my hearing aid on. I'll never bake again."

"Hey, Biney," said Allen, who was standing with their mother and Maria. "Don't blame the cookies. It was the timer that gave you trouble."

"That's a problem we'll have to work on," their father said. "Don't give up."

Biney nibbled at her food during the evening meal. She paid little attention to her family. As her mom served the ice cream, Biney noticed Allen wriggling restlessly in his chair.

"Okay, let's have some of the burnt cookies," he said, grinning.

"Allen!" scolded the parents.

Biney jerked her chair back and left the table, scowling at Allen. She headed for her bedroom and the solace of her favorite chair. She felt miserable. Recalling the events of the past several days, she realized that all of them had happened because she couldn't hear. She still wasn't sure what to do about the hearing aid, but she vowed she was not going to cry anymore. It didn't solve any of her problems.

About an hour later, Biney felt a tap on her shoulder. Her dad stood in front of her.

"Look at this, Biney." He opened a brown paper bag, took out a timer, and showed it to her.

"Look," he said as he set the timer for one minute. "Put it in your pocket and wait."

After the minute was up, the buzzer rang.

"Can you feel the vibration when it buzzes?"

Biney nodded.

"When the hearing aid alone can't help you, this timer will help, especially when you have to go to another room. Bake me some cookies when I come back from my next trip," her father urged. "And use the timer. Promise?"

Biney reluctantly agreed, still not sure she wanted to try again.

"Promise?" her dad said again, persistently.

"All right, I promise," Biney responded, more firmly.

"Biney," he continued, "when something goes wrong, do we give up?"

"No," muttered Biney. "I know we're supposed to try to solve our problems. You made that clear a long time ago."

"Okay, then. If you can't solve your problem one way,

please be sure to try to find an answer in a different way. Today you found out that the timer on the stove is not strong enough. This new timer may not work, either. We may have to look for something else, but give it a try."

Biney's mother came into the room. "Pat wants to talk to you on the phone."

"You talk to her, Mom," Biney requested. "I hate the phone. The hearing aid doesn't help me."

"Pat wants to see if you can understand her," continued Mom. "Come on, I expect you to give it a try."

Biney went downstairs and turned the switch on her hearing aid to the telephone microphone. Then she picked up the receiver and said, "Hi, Pat."

"Hi," said Pat.

"Why does Pat insist on trying to talk to me on the telephone?" Biney wondered, getting angrier and angrier. *"All I can hear is a warbling sound and I can't do anything about it. I hate coming to the phone. This hearing aid feels like a big lump wedged in my ear, and it's making it throb. I feel like tearing the hearing aid out of my ear and never wearing it again."* "I can't understand you at all, Pat. Bye."

Biney raced upstairs to her room, took off her hearing aid, and slumped in the wicker chair. Enough was enough.

A little while later Pat walked into Biney's room. She sat down on the footstool and looked at Biney. Placing her hand on her forehead above her glasses, she looked around like she was searching for something.

"Where is my happy-go-lucky, cheerful friend?" asked Pat. "Poof! She's gone. Maybe she's hiding."

Pat walked to the bay window, lifted up the window seat and peered inside. "Where is she?"

Moving across the room toward the bed, Pat got on her hands and knees and looked under the bed. Turning to

Biney, she worriedly exclaimed, "Where is she? Where's Biney? Oh, there you are. Are you Biney? Where's that teasing grin?"

"Stop it, Pat," said Biney. "I'm in no mood for playing. Anyway, you can't see me all the way across the room. You're nearly blind. Even with those glasses."

"I can pretend, can't I?" asked Pat, sitting on the footstool facing Biney. "You don't seem happy. Could you understand me at all on the telephone?"

"No," answered Biney. "I've quit wearing my hearing aid. It's not helping me enough."

"How do you know?" asked Pat. "You haven't had it very long."

"I've had nothing but trouble since I got it. I couldn't hear the timer. I couldn't understand anyone on the phone. All the hearing aid does for me is make sounds louder; it doesn't make words clearer. I can't understand the sounds I hear. It is not helping me and I hate it. And because I can't understand anybody, I don't want to see anybody. Go away."

"Okay, Biney, I'll go," said Pat. "I came over here to ask you to come over to my house tomorrow. Why don't we talk about it then?"

Even though she still had a strong desire not to see or talk to anyone, Biney realized that Pat seemed to understand her.

"All right," Biney answered. "I'll come, but I won't wear the hearing aid. I'll be drawing in the morning. How about at one. Uh,...is Gene is going to be there?"

"No. He and Carl are going fishing and my dad is away. That's why I am asking you over."

The next afternoon, Maria took Biney to Pat's house.

"I'll walk home, Maria," said Biney.

"If you change your mind, call me. All you have to say is 'Come.'"

Biney nodded.

One wall in Pat's family room was covered with a large map. Glancing at the bookcase Biney noticed two smooth carved dolphins. One looked ready to dip into the water, while the other was ready to come up. "I've never seen these before. Where did they come from?"

"My uncle is in the Navy," said Pat. "He travels all over the world. The dolphins are from New Guinea." She pointed to the map showing where it was located. "Those masks under the map are from Australia, and the bell is from Bali. Gene wants to join the Navy, too."

Biney noticed a computer sitting on a small table near a window. "This is Gene's new computer," Pat told her while she inserted a flat disk into the disk drive and typed a few words.

"I'm honest John Smith," appeared on the screen. "I run a Swap 'n Shop Store. I buy and sell all kinds of things—furniture and junk. Do you want to sell anything? Type yes or no."

"Go ahead, type yes," Pat urged.

Biney typed in her answer and the computer responded with, "What do you want to sell?"

"Bracelet," typed Biney.

"Yes, I will buy it for one dollar," came the reply.

"Hey, it's worth more than that," protested Biney.

"What else do you wish to sell?"

Pat wrote, "House."

"I will swap a cat for the house," wrote the computer. "If you don't want to swap, I will buy the house for five dollars. Anything else?"

Biney giggled.

"Hey, you're gypping me," Pat hollered at the computer. "You know, Biney, the computer uses random numbers. You can never predict what price it will offer."

Biney typed in, "Gold thimble."

"Oh yes, I will pay ten thousand for it."

"What!" exclaimed Biney, clapping her hand to her mouth. "No thimble is worth that much, but I'll take it."

"What did it say?" asked Pat, squinting with her eyes very close to the screen. "I can't read it."

Biney looked at Pat in disbelief. "Pat, what's the matter with you? Where are your glasses? You know you can't read without them."

"Oh, I left them over there, on the desk," Pat replied. "They just don't help me enough."

Biney looked blankly at Pat, then suddenly recognized she was hearing her own excuse for not using her hearing aid. She angrily got up from the chair, accidentally bumping the computer. The words disappeared from the screen. Startled, Biney stared at the computer. "Did I ruin it?" she asked, her voice trembling. "Did I ruin the computer?"

"Oh, don't worry about it. I only have to type a few commands to put it back on the screen," Pat said confidently.

Pat typed a few words. Nothing appeared. After a few more unsuccessful attempts, she declared, "Maybe we did ruin it. Gosh, Gene is going to be really mad."

"When is he coming home?"

"Around five."

"I'll come back then," Biney promised. "I want to know if I ruined it."

Biney left Pat's house wondering how much it would cost to have the computer repaired. She had some money with her to buy the vase at the antique shop. *"If I buy the vase now, I won't have much left to pay for fixing the computer,"* she thought. *"What should I do? I haven't*

77

drawn enough cards to sell more to Mrs. Caldwell.'' Biney kept thinking all the way to the antique shop.

When she arrived at the antique shop, Biney saw that the vase was still on top of the rolltop desk. She stood at the window debating with herself—should she buy the vase or save her money for the repair?

Biney looked in the window for the woman who had made her leave the antique shop the last time. She saw only one person browsing in the store. Then she spotted the saleswoman dusting some ceramic dishes in the back. *"Oh, well,''* Biney decided, *"I'll worry about the computer later.''*

Biney entered the antique shop, picked up the vase, and looked at the tag. The price was the same. She took the vase to the saleswoman. The woman looked up, frowned, and said a lot of words Biney couldn't understand.

Biney guessed she was fussing about her being a kid, so she placed the vase on the counter, reached in her purse, and thrust her money toward the woman.

"I want to buy it," Biney said slowly, in an effort to say the words clearly. Not sure if the saleswoman had understood her, Biney repeated herself.

The woman stared at her, counted the money, and then nodded.

As Biney started to leave with the vase, the sales woman grabbed her arm, pointed to the counter, and beckoned with her finger. Puzzled, Biney followed her to the counter. The woman took the vase, wrapped it carefully in some old newspapers, and put it in a bag.

"Thank you," said Biney, feeling better about the saleswoman. "Thank you, very much."

The old woman nodded, grinning. With a questioning look on her face, she placed her hand behind her own ear.

Biney nodded, "Yes, I'm hearing impaired," and waved good-bye.

When Biney arrived home an hour later, she saw her mother's car parked in front of the garage. Wanting to surprise her mother, Biney opened the front door quietly and tiptoed to the door of the family room. She felt the vibration of someone walking on the upstairs floor, so she quickly unwrapped the vase and put it on top of the television. She stuffed the newspapers and bag in the wastebasket and rushed back to the front door. Just then her mother appeared at the top of the steps.

"Biney, I'm glad you're home," she said as she walked down the stairs. "I have some news for you."

"What?" Biney asked.

"Come on, let's talk in the family room," her mother responded. "This will be our chance to make plans.

"Maria called. Her parents are having a party Saturday night. They're going to entertain guests from all over the world. Maria thought you would enjoy helping them, especially with serving refreshments. Maria will pick you up in the morning to talk with you about it, and tomorrow night we will get you a new dress. . . ."

Biney watched her mother looking at the vase. The startled surprise and the puzzled look stayed on her mother's face.

"Wh—where did that vase come from?" her mother stammered.

"I bought it," answered Biney. "Since I can't ever bring Grandma's vase back, it was the best I could do."

"Oh, Biney, sweetheart," her mom said as she reached over to hug her. "There was no need for you to do that. I didn't say anything about it because I knew it was an accident. I see now how you must have worried about it. Thank you. Thank you very much." She hugged Biney again.

Early that evening, Biney reluctantly put her hearing aid in her ear as she prepared to walk to Pat's home. She told her mother where she was going and promised to be home in time for dinner. Thirty minutes later, as she approached her friend's house, Gene came running out to meet her.

"Biney, Pat told me you were coming. I was looking for you to tell you to please go home. Dad is drunk. Sometimes he gets real angry and yells at us. I didn't want you to be surprised or scared by him."

"Oh, thanks. But I want to know if the computer is broken," Biney told him, not moving.

"No, it isn't," he answered. "The program was wiped out, but I can do it over. Please go."

For the first time, Biney looked at his eyes, which were a startling blue. "Are you sure the computer's okay?" she asked. "Because, I was going to have it repaired."

"No, really, it's all right."

Biney stared at his eyes. All these years she had focused her attention on his lips, she had never noticed he had such pretty eyes. But there was something else. Those eyes showed something. What was it? Concern? Worry? She hadn't realized eyes could be so expressive.

Gene's father came out of the kitchen door.

"Go, Biney. You shouldn't be here," Gene insisted, pushing her to make her move quickly. Then he ran back toward his father.

Biney rushed down the block, being careful to stay on the sidewalk near the highway. *"What pretty blue eyes,"* she repeated to herself. Barely watching the cars going by, she crossed the street. She stopped on the opposite sidewalk, stunned by another thought. *"Gene didn't call me dummy! Maybe he was too concerned about my safety."*

10

The next morning, Maria picked up Biney and they drove to the condominium where she lived with her parents. Biney counted ten rows of windows as they walked toward the tall building. At either end of the building, miniature rectangular roofs hung over the bay windows at each level, providing a slight curve to the building's otherwise stream-lined appearance.

Biney and Maria entered the large lobby and walked over to a waiting elevator. When they got in, Maria pushed five. Biney felt the elevator rise; she felt an odd sensation, like she was floating in the air. When the elevator stopped, a few people left and others came on. When it started moving again, Biney noticed that her hearing aid did not pick up the sound of whatever it was that made the elevator move again. When the doors opened on the fifth floor, Maria walked out ahead of Biney and led her down the long hall toward her door.

"Welcome to my home!" Maria announced as she opened the door and led Biney through the octagonal foyer to the living room. .

Biney stood in the living room doorway, trying to take in everything. She caught the faint smell of an orange plant blending with the appetizing aroma of cookies baking somewhere in the apartment.

"Come in, sit down," Maria invited, plopping down on one of the sofas.

"I love this room, Maria. It's inviting, but it looks foreign, too."

"Well, we've lived in several different countries and we've traveled a lot. But we've settled here now—for good, I hope."

Biney sat down on the cream-colored sofa facing Maria. A carved statue of a mother and baby made of polished black wood sat in the middle of the coffee table. Biney gently touched its smooth surface. Flanking the carving were two very small trees, each not more than eight inches tall.

"Those trees—they are trees, aren't they?" questioned Biney. "They're so little."

"They're old, too," Maria responded. "One hundred years old. They're called bonsai trees. They come from Japan. The Japanese know how to make them stay little."

Drawn by the opened doors to the terrace, Biney walked onto the terrace and searched for her house. She finally spotted the chimney and most of the roof hidden behind the cedar trees.

"Oh look, you can see the cliff," she exclaimed. "The rocks are so white against the leaves on the trees."

Maria nodded. "Yes, the cliff is beautiful."

Returning to the living room, Biney noticed three eggs on the mantel of the fireplace. "What are those?" she asked.

"That is my collection of eggs. They are made of gold, silver, diamonds, and other stones. In the early 1900s, Czar

Nicholas II of Russia gave the eggs to his wife and other members of the royal family. Peter Faberge was the jeweler who made the eggs. His eggs are very famous now. Try and say his name, Biney, Fab-er-jay.''

Maria repeated the word until Biney said it correctly. ''Look, the Faberge eggs have surprises on the inside, like miniature pictures or an arrangement of gem stones.''

''Oh, they're so pretty,'' exclaimed Biney. ''Where did you get them?''

''My dad and I looked for them when we traveled in different countries,'' answered Maria. ''Come on, let's find Dora.''

Dora, the Phillippi's housekeeper, was in the kitchen transferring cookies from the cookie sheet to the cooling racks. Maria introduced Biney and Dora to each other. Biney liked her immediately. Dora picked up a cookie and offered it to Biney.

Maria waved to get Biney's attention. ''Biney, we need to know just where to put the trays, and we have to practice serving food to guests. Pretend like there are guests in the living room and do what Dora and I do so you will know what to expect tomorrow night,'' Maria instructed.

Trailing them, Biney picked up an empty tray from the buffet in the dining room, walked into the living room, and went around the room pretending to serve guests. After she had made the rounds, she returned the ''empty'' tray to the kitchen and picked up a full one in the dining room.

''Now, you do it by yourself,'' said Maria. ''We're going into the living room and pretend to be guests.''

Biney picked up a tray and entered the living room. She headed toward Dora, who was sitting on one of the sofas, and bent down to bring the tray to the proper position.

Dora daintily reached for an hors d'oeuvre. ''Thank you,'' she said. ''Hey, wait a minute,'' she called, just as

Biney began to leave her. "Can't I have any more?"

Surprised, Biney brought the tray back.

Dora laughed. "I was just kidding. Can't you smile? Come on, you're taking this too seriously."

Biney grinned. "Sure." Whirling around toward Maria, she danced with poise, holding the tray high. "How's that?" Biney asked, giggling and curtsying at the same time.

"Now, you're lively. But no dancing tomorrow night," cautioned Maria, laughing at the same time. "When they say 'thank you,' all you need to say is 'you're welcome.' Try it one more time."

Biney practiced once again.

"That's great; you won't have any problem," Maria assured her.

Biney's mother drove her to Maria's Saturday evening. Unlike the previous day, when there had been only a few cars in the parking lot, the lot now was full. Biney nervously shifted in her seat as her mother tried to find a parking space. Once they parked, Biney and her mother walked across the parking lot to the building entrance. Biney noticed a car with its steering wheel on the right side.

"Look at that steering wheel, Mom."

"That's an English car," answered her mother. "You know, there'll be people from different countries at the party tonight. Make sure you watch their lips carefully when they talk to you. Biney, you look wonderful in your new dress. I wish I could stay and watch you serve."

"Thanks," Biney answered, her voice shaking. "Gee, Mom, I'm nervous."

"You'll be fine once you begin serving the guests."

When Biney first walked into the Phillippi's foyer, she was surprised by a strange, undulating sound. As she neared the living room, she realized the noise was coming from the guests talking to each other. She turned down the volume of her hearing aid and went to look for Maria. She found her in the dining room getting a tray of hors d'oeuvres. Biney picked up a tray, too, and followed Maria into the living room. The sound of so many different voices became more penetrating as they walked into the living room with their trays. *"At least, I can turn off my hearing aid if I can't stand the noise,"* Biney told herself.

Before serving the guests, Biney looked at the food to make sure she knew what was on the tray. She didn't want to be embarrassed if a guest asked her what something was. There were slices of cucumber with sour cream and caviar on top, miniature mushroom and beef turnovers, spinach and cheese strudel, and spiced shrimp. As she carried the tray to each guest, she watched their lips closely for the "thank you" most of them seemed to say. She nodded briefly after each one, replying, "You're welcome."

One of the guests grabbed Biney's arm and said something to her. Biney watched the woman's lips and tried to catch any of her words, but she couldn't understand her. Biney felt helpless. She stood for a second, looking at the woman, and then turned away from her puzzled expression to serve other guests. Biney became more and more uncomfortable with the loud noise in the room and the uncertainty of what the guests were saying. She felt like an alien from space. She wasn't a part of the group, yet she was, too.

When Biney went to the dining room to pick up another tray of hors d'oeuvres, she saw Dora carrying out platters of food and placing them on the dining room table. Biney took a deep breath of the unfamiliar, yet tantalizing, aromas of the meal about to be served. The table looked beautiful. Right in the middle of the table sat a swan carved of ice.

Maria had told her earlier the swan would remain frozen for at least two hours before it began to melt. The swan centerpiece looked so beautiful, Biney could hardly tear herself away to serve the guests.

Biney continued making her rounds with the hors d'oeuvre tray. When she came to two men standing in the doorway leading to the terrace, she noticed that their voices boomed above everyone else's. The two men jostled each other with their arms, making Biney wonder if they were angry. As she walked slowly toward them, one of the men lashed his arms out sideways, hitting Biney's tray and scattering food all over the carpet.

Several other men in the room crowded around the two men. Maria's father grabbed the two men and spoke loudly to them. To Biney, his voice sounded like the heavy, rapid vibration of the drums in a parade.

Biney felt a tap on her shoulder. She looked up and saw Maria point to the scattered food. Together they picked up the mess. One of the men who had been fighting reached over to Biney, said a few words, and pulled out a hundred-dollar bill. He placed it in her hand. Biney looked at the bill in amazement. She vigorously shook her head and pushed it back in his hand. She rushed from the room to escape him, to escape the noisy guests, and to turn off her hearing aid. Leaning against the wall, she cradled her head inside her elbow and gritted her teeth to control her feeling of loathing for those men.

A few minutes later, Maria found Biney in the hall. She grabbed her and hugged her. "Come on, I'm taking you home," Maria said. "The guests are lining up for dinner. We've done our part."

Half an hour later, back at home, Biney started to get out of Maria's car.

"Wait a minute, Biney," Maria requested. "Let's talk a little."

86

Biney slid back into the seat and closed the car door.

"I think you thought those men were angry," Maria began. "They weren't, they were just poking fun at each other. When the man realized he knocked your tray down, money was his way of saying he was sorry."

"Mom warned me long ago not to accept money from any strangers," said Biney. "It may have been all right, but I couldn't do it."

Maria nodded. "In spite of that, I want you to know you did a super job tonight."

"Thanks," answered Biney, opening the car door. "Most of the time things went smoothly."

"Here's a little something for helping us," Maria said, handing Biney a gift-wrapped box. "See you Monday."

Biney stood in front of her house and watched Maria's car disappear down the driveway. Turning with reluctance toward the house, she noticed a light in the family room. She decided not to tell her folks about the mishap.

Biney's mother was curled up on the sofa reading a book. Her father was sitting in the chair by the fireplace smoking his pipe. "How was it?" he asked.

"It was okay," Biney answered. She described the guests, their unusual clothes, and the food. As she talked to them, she unwrapped her gift.

"Oh wow; this is great!" Biney exclaimed, as she twisted open the tube of dusty pink lipstick. "Maria put a little of hers on me tonight. I really felt grown up, but when I left the party, I felt like a little girl, again. There are too many things going on that I don't understand."

"Give yourself time," her mom encouraged.

"I think I'll go to bed. I'm tired."

"We understand." said Dad, "I just want to tell you how nice you look with your hair short, especially in your new dress."

"Thanks, Dad," said Biney, surprised that he noticed her hair.

11

Biney took off her new dress and hung it carefully in her wardrobe. She put on her favorite nightgown and then sat down in the bay window to reflect on the evening's events. She pictured the women in their beautiful gowns and the men in their tuxedos and wondered what they had been talking about. Despite the steady drone of conversations, Biney still thought that the two men had been arguing about something. She wondered what the guests had said to her after their "thank yous." *"Some of them looked bewildered when I didn't respond to their questions or whatever they said,"* she recalled. *"I guess not knowing what to do and moving to other guests didn't solve the problem. But, what should I have done? Make a comment? No, that would have shown them that I didn't understand them."*

Biney thought back to times when people hadn't understood her. She remembered the puzzled reaction she got from the drugstore waitress when she ordered a milk shake. *"Tonight, I had that same nervous feeling that I had when I rushed out of the drugstore. Carl told me the waitress just asked what size milk shake I wanted. And he encouraged me* to tell the waitress that I couldn't hear. What if I had told her? Would the waitress still have thought I was dumb? Gene always calls me dumb. Maybe I am dumb. But, the girl in school who always gets bad grades is called dumb, and I don't feel like her. I also don't feel like the guests at the party who could talk, laugh—and even poke fun at each other.''

Tears streamed down Biney's cheeks as she realized how different she was and how alone she felt. "The only people I can communicate with are the people who know me well," she moaned to herself.

As she got up for a tissue, more memories came flooding back. Like the time she had trouble at the library because she couldn't understand the librarian. And the time when she asked Allen what the man said on the television and all she got was a "never mind" and a broken vase. Biney threw the sodden tissue toward the wastebasket and pulled out another handful. New tears quickly soaked through the tissues. She tossed them toward the wastebasket and reached for another bunch.

"When I'm home, everyone treats me like I can't think for myself," she continued. "Then, when I try to do things on my own, like walking home alone, my parents get furious. But look what happened when I tried to make the cookies by myself—I was a complete failure!

"I wonder if the hearing aid can help me. I don't want people to see it, though. Then, they'll feel sorry for me. They'll probably think I'm not capable of taking care of myself. I don't know what to do. Even Pat thinks my excuse about not wanting to wear the hearing aid was flimsy, but it seems like the hearing aid doesn't help, all it does is cause trouble.''

Biney threw the tissues into the wastebasket. She rocked herself back and forth, trying to get rid of the miserable feeling she had. She looked out of the bay window at the peaceful scene below. The low-hanging moon spread a soft glow on the trees and the ground. She noticed that the tree shadows on the ground were fading. She glanced up at the moon. The clouds shifted gradually from the edge of the moon toward the center. Exhausted, she fell into her bed.

Biney came down for breakfast late Monday morning.

"Well good morning, Biney," Maria said. "Have you recovered from the party?"

Biney nodded. "Uh huh. I overslept this morning, but I think it's still early enough for me to draw at the top of the cliff before the kids come to the park to play. I really like the feel of being part of the woods when it's cool and quiet up there."

"Hey, can I go with you?" asked Allen.

"Sure," responded Biney. "Come on. We'll go as soon as I get my art stuff."

"I'll get my cars and shovel," added Allen.

As Biney walked with Allen down the hill toward the old maple tree, she said, "Let's see if there's anything in the knothole." And there was. Biney took out a note that read, "Who am I?"

"Hey, Biney," Allen exclaimed. "You've got a secret admirer. Who do you think it is?"

"I think it's Carl. You know, Gene's friend. Have you seen anyone bringing any notes?"

"No."

"Oh well; come on, let's go up to the cliff."

Ten minutes later, Biney was drawing while Allen dug with his shovel in the dirt around the roots of a nearby tree.

Biney broke off a branch full of bright red berries from a spicebush and inhaled the wonderful smell. "Allen, do you remember drinking tea with Grandma?" she asked her

90

brother.

"Yes," he replied, "but, I was just barely old enough to remember her."

"I remember her really well. The spicebush smell always reminds me of her," Biney said as she arranged the branch against the bush. *"This will make a perfect card,"* she told herself.

Allen continued to dig deeper and deeper. "I'm making a tunnel," he announced as he tossed the dirt sideways. He folded a small bandanna to form the roof of the tunnel. Moving a car toward the tunnel, he reached in halfway and pulled the car out the opposite side with his other hand. But he couldn't move the cars in and out without disturbing the cover. In frustration, he picked up the bandanna and tucked it in his pants pocket.

Biney chuckled to herself over Allen's frustration. She leaned against the tree trunk and enjoyed the cool breeze ruffling her hair. School would start in just three days and already she felt the changing weather. Some of the leaves were beginning to turn colors. Acorns lay all around her on the ground. The sun's rays, not so blistering hot anymore, slanted at a different angle through the trees, as if preparing the trees for the coming cold weather. *"Only one card left,"* she thought, waking herself from her daydream.

Suddenly dirt flew up in Biney's face and scattered all over her card. She tried brushing the dirt away with her hand, but it smeared the picture of the spicebush. "Oh no," she cried, staring at the ruined card.

Dirt flew at Biney again. This time Biney turned around and saw Allen throwing the dirt over his shoulder, absorbed in his digging.

"Allen!" Biney exclaimed. "Quit throwing the dirt. It's landing on my cards. You've ruined my picture."

Allen looked up with surprise. "I didn't mean to do it. I'm sorry. Don't be angry, Biney."

Just at that moment, Gene appeared next to Allen. "Yeah, that's right, dummy," he said. "Don't pick on Allen."

Startled, Biney just stared at Gene. *"Where did he come from?"* she wondered. She tossed down her pencil and clipboard, scrambled to her feet, and glared at him.

"Uh oh, look who's angry," Gene said laughing. "Don't look at me; Allen threw the dirt."

"Quit it," hollered Biney. She moved toward him.

"Uh oh, I'm scared," Gene teased, wriggling back and forth keeping just out of Biney's reach. "Ha, ha, you can't even catch up with me."

Biney ran faster, but Gene's long legs still kept him out of reach. Then he slipped.

12

Biney stood, horrified, as Gene slipped off the cliff. He frantically grabbed at the branches of the nearby trees; his fingers snatched at a twig. As it broke, he tumbled downward. He clawed uselessly at grass, at dirt, at pebbles, at anything at all.

Biney stood paralyzed, feeling helpless. Her face was distorted with the same panic Gene's showed as his fingers lost hold of the edge. Allen, screaming with fright, ran to the edge and looked down. Biney hesitated, but the fear of what was happening to Gene moved her to the edge, too.

They watched Gene grab at the grass and dirt as he slid down the wall of the cliff. Then, he bumped into a small tree sticking out at an angle from the sheer wall. As it broke, Gene shrieked in terror.

Rooted to the top of the bluff, Biney clung to a tree to support her shaking body as she watched Gene's body bump against the sharp rocks in the wall.

After what seemed an eternity, Gene finally landed on the ledge halfway down the steep incline. His arms and legs dangled like a rag doll's. With a frantic motion he reached for a stunted evergreen tree at the back of the ledge. At the same time, his body slid toward the edge. Biney caught her breath as she watched Gene scrambling to keep his legs from sliding off.

"Pull, Gene," shouted Allen. "Pull!"

Gene grasped the tree and pulled his body toward the back of the ledge. Biney could see him straining every muscle in his neck and arms. With one last painful effort, Gene rolled over onto his back and clasped his arms around the tree. His legs flopped out to the sides, and Biney saw that one was oddly twisted.

As Gene lay motionless on the ground, thoughts began racing through Biney's mind—*"Gene is lying so still. Why doesn't he move? His leg must be broken. I shouldn't have chased him. He's so white. Come on, Gene, move. Maybe he can't. Is his body broken?"*—that terrible thought jolted Biney into action.

"Come on, Allen. We've got to get down there. Oh, I hope he's not dead. He's got to be all right."

"Oh no, he better not be dead."

Biney and Allen grabbed the nearby tree branches for support while they climbed down the steep side trail. Other branches whipped their faces. Biney slipped and bumped against a huge boulder.

"Hey, are you okay?" asked Allen, stopping to help her up.

"Yeah, come on, keep going," answered Biney. "But carefully."

Halfway down, Biney turned to an almost invisible trail that extended to the ledge. The trail was seldom used because the ledge was not considered safe. She prayed it was strong enough to hold Gene. As they reached the ledge, Biney could feel her heart pounding in her aching chest. She was breathing heavily and the breath caught in her throat, drying it out.

Biney reached Gene first. She stood in front of him, her legs quivering. In an effort to stop the shaking, she stiffened her legs, but discovered she was trembling all over. Looking at Allen's face, she saw the same shock she felt. *"I must not let him see I'm scared, too,"* she cautioned herself. Just as Biney moved toward him, Gene moved.

"Ohhh," moaned Gene, moving his head sideways. The blood from the gash on his forehead dribbled down toward his ear.

Biney's heart leaped. "Gene, don't move," she said. Gene opened his eyes and she put her hand on his shoulder.

"What are you doing?" Gene exclaimed, moving to get up. "Ouch." Surprised, he moved his leg again. "Oww; that hurts," he cried.

Biney cleared her throat and talked slowly so Allen and Gene wouldn't hear how nervous she was. She motioned for Allen to come nearer. "Gene, lie still," she ordered, her voice quaking as she wiped the blood from his forehead with Allen's bandanna. "I think your leg is broken."

Biney didn't like the vague look in Gene's eyes as he stared at her. The look made her feel uncomfortable. *"How can Allen and I get him home? We can't,"* she realized. *"I better get Maria."*

Determined not to show how nervous she felt, Biney spoke firmly. "Allen, put your hand on Gene's shoulder and keep him down. I'm getting Maria." She looked at him closely and watched him swallow hard several times. "Can you do it?"

"Yes," Allen responded hesitantly. "I think so."

Biney jogged down the trail leading to the pond. She struggled to keep up her pace while she climbed the hill toward the house. Her chest heaved in and out as she tried to get more air past her dry throat into her lungs. She stopped by an oak tree halfway up the hill, breathed rapidly to build up her air supply, and then jogged again until she reached the twin doors of the old house.

She ran through the front hall to the kitchen, where she thought Maria would be, but she wasn't there. Biney tried to stay calm as she rushed into the dining room and living room and then across the hall to the family room calling Maria's name. She went upstairs and looked in each room along the upstairs hall.

Maria was gone.

As Biney walked downstairs, she pictured Gene lying on the ledge in pain. "What now?" she asked out loud. She sat on the bottom step and tried to think of an answer. "The neighbors are too far away. Besides, I don't think I can run any more," she observed. Getting up, she noticed the emergency call number on the wall by the telephone. She stared at the number a long moment.

"No way! I can't talk on the phone, especially because I can't understand anybody." Biney paced back and forth in the hall and concentrated on how to get help without the phone. But her mind remained a blank; the phone seemed to be the only answer. Her throat tightened at the thought of making a call. She placed her hand on the receiver, lifted it, hesitated, then put it back down. Her heart thumped wildly.

"What should I say? How will I understand them?" she wondered. But, the scene of Gene lying on the ledge tormented her. She had to do something. She grabbed a sheet of paper and wrote down what she would say. Then, she ran upstairs to get her hearing aid and returned as fast as she could. She adjusted her hearing aid to the telephone switch, firmly lifted the receiver, and dialed 911.

She waited until she faintly heard the phone stop ringing and then began speaking. "This is Biney Richmond. I am hearing impaired. I will not be able to understand you. This

96

is an emergency." Then she gave a description of the accident and the directions to her house.

"I am going to repeat. This is Biney Richmond. I am hearing impaired. . . ." When she replaced the receiver, she was shaking, but she knew she had done her best. She thought over the message she had given. *"Maybe Pat and Mom were right. The aid is good for something, after all. I couldn't have made that call without it."* For the first time in a long time, she felt good about herself.

Biney stood on the porch waiting for the rescue squad van to appear. She decided she would call again in thirty minutes if no one came. To her relief, the van appeared in fifteen minutes. It stopped near the porch steps. The driver got out and walked toward Biney. "Miss Richmond?" he asked.

"Yes sir," Biney replied.

"Can you show us where your friend is?"

"Sure. Follow me," Biney said.

"Okay, let's go." the driver said, as he and another man pulled a stretcher from the van.

13

Biney and Allen waited nervously in the hospital emergency room. Biney looked at the clock again and again. It seemed as if the doctor was working a long time on Gene. She hoped nothing else was wrong besides the broken leg. "We've been waiting almost two hours," Biney said to Allen. "What do you think they're doing in there?" But, before Allen could answer, a nurse wheeled Gene into the room.

"Hey, dummy," Gene called. His right leg was covered with a cast that extended from his toes to his thigh.

Biney glared at him. "Dummy?"

"Whoa," said Gene, covering his face with his hands as if to protect himself. He wheeled himself closer and put his hands on Biney's shoulders. "I was just kidding. Don't you know that?" he asked.

"Not always. Sometimes it seems that's the only thing you call me. But just because I can't hear doesn't mean I'm stupid. I'm not! And I can talk, too. So don't call me dummy anymore," she pleaded.

"Biney, it took courage for you to climb down to the ledge to help me. And I know it was hard for you to call for help. Thanks," Gene said. "I have a habit of calling you dummy. I admit it's a bad habit. I'll try really hard not to do it anymore. But give me time. And when I forget, remember I don't mean it. Okay?"

Biney, drawn by his pretty blue eyes and his muscular shoulders and arms, felt the words catch in her throat. Afraid to trust her voice, she nodded shyly.

"What's the matter?" asked Gene. "Got a frog in your throat?"

Biney shook her head. "Not this time, Mickey Mouse."

"Does Mickey Mouse need to leave more notes at the maple tree?" asked Gene with an impish look.

Biney caught her breath. *"Gene left me the notes!"* Biney suddenly realized. *"All this time the teasing really meant he liked me!"*

"You thought it was Carl, didn't you?"

Biney nodded. "Thank you, especially for the flower."

Biney's parents came into the emergency room. "Biney, you were marvelous," her mother declared. "The rescue squad captain told us what you did—climbing out on the ledge, taking charge, using the phone, everything!"

"You were great," said her dad. "We're very proud of you! You really have grown up, Biney. How do you feel?"

"Pretty good," Biney acknowledged.

"I guess that means you don't need me anymore," Maria added.

"Oh, yes I do," exclaimed Biney. "Maybe, I did all right this time, but I still have a lot to learn."

Mr. and Mrs. Sullivan and Pat arrived at the hospital a few minutes later. They walked over to Gene and hugged him. Then, Gene's parents turned to Biney and Allen, shook their hands, and thanked them for getting Gene to the hospital.

Pat hugged Biney. "I'm going to talk to you on the

phone yet. And I expect to get results!"

"Maybe—with time," answered Biney.

One of the nurses came out and stood in back of the wheelchair, ready to roll Gene outside to the car.

"Wait," Gene requested, holding up his hand. "Biney, when I can take long walks again, I want to take you to the drugstore for a milk shake. Okay? Here's a pen. If you sign your name on my cast, that means you promise you'll go with me."

Smiling, Biney took the pen and signed her name.

For more books about hearing loss
write to

Gallaudet University Press
800 Florida Avenue NE
Washington, DC 20002
800-672-6720 ext. 5488 (V/TDD)